CONTENTS

This series is dedicated to my five.

You are my everything.

Fern Day is barely holding it together most days. The single, fully-human mom of a fifteen-year-old-shifter-with-an-attitude has no time for herself. Her life is chaos, she's a hot mess, and her daughter is her first priority.

Sunkissed Key's handsome pediatrician sure is tempting, though. When he offers to teach her daughter how to handle her animal side, Fern can't refuse. But that's not his only offer Fern can't refuse.

Harrison Daniels knows Fern is his the moment he lays eyes on her. He also knows she's not ready to learn about shifter mating. She'll only view him as another responsibility, and lord knows she's juggling enough of those already. That child of hers is an unholy terror.

Harrison has his work cut out for him. He not only has to convince Fern that he's in her life forever, he also has to gain the approval of her spawn from hell. Good thing Harrison never backs down from a challenge. Bring it on.

FERN

Sandra Fergus kicked off her modesty sheet and lay butt naked on my massage table, mooing like a cow while I dug firmly into the muscles of her back. When the door to my massage room flew open and a cold breeze blew over Sandra's southern bits, her moos turned to squawks and she startled, flailing wildly for cover. What her flailing fists ended up latching onto was my shirt. With a fist full of my faux silk button-down, she pulled me over the table and on top of her, making me a human shield. Sandra was a muscular woman. I was not. I had no hope of getting free until she released me.

I still couldn't see who opened the door. For all I knew, I was being used as a shield against an irate client gone postal. I'd never heard of a shooting in a salon, but there seemed to be so many irrational sorts of shootings in the news lately that my mind went straight to that scenario. Lord knew that salons, in general, saw their share of unhappy clients. But surely, crooked acrylics, faded hair color, or loose eyelash extensions were no reasons for a client to resort to gun violence. Neither was massage dissatisfaction. But one never knew these days.

I panicked and, screaming, reached out for something to shield myself with. It just so happened that what I found was Sandra's impressively augmented boob. My hand latched on tightly a second before my brain registered that the soft, squishy thing was a C-sized, semi-silicone, female breast. Had my brain been only a split second faster in its processing, I would've stopped myself from doing the inadvertent boob-grab for cover and instead just gone out like a hero. How did one apologize for boob-grabbing?

A moment passed. Another. Finally, wondering why a hail of bullets hadn't rained down on my little massage room yet, I dared a glance over my shoulder. My moody, fifteen-year-old daughter, Kinsley, stood in the doorway scowling. Jammie appeared behind Kinsley. As she stood witness to what I imagined would go down in history as one of my all-time most mortifying moments, her jaw dropped and her colorfully made up eyes flew open so wide, it looked as though her eyeballs might fall right out of their sockets.

Jammie owned the salon, and I was her newest hire, replacing the recently retired masseuse, Frannie. She probably should've fired me on the spot. Not Jammie, though. No, Jammie just threw her head back and laughed until tears ran down her cheeks and she could barely stand. She laughed so hard, I worried she was going to throw her back out.

When I realized my fingers were still digging into Sandra's tit, I released my grasp with a couple of quick pats of apology to her tender flesh and tried to shift my weight back to my feet to stand up. Sandra still had an unyielding grip on my shirt, though, and I was splayed across her body in a way that, no matter how hard I wiggled, I couldn't maneuver myself backward, or forward. When she came to her senses, in one quick motion, she released me and turned to hide. The move lent forward momentum to my body and sent my upper half shooting off the table, headfirst toward the floor. Before my head hit, I caught myself with my hands, balanced precariously, then slowly and carefully slid the rest of my body off the table in a snakelike slither that made the entire situation all the more awkward.

Livid, Sandra began screaming at me.

She screamed at me, I screamed at Kinsley, and Jammie was gasping for breath in between howls and cackles.

When I finally managed to get to my feet, I pointed a stiff arm at my daughter and ordered her to wait outside for me. Sandra was on the other side of the massage table making a feeble attempt to hide her girlie bits with her hands. I wasn't sure whether she was aware that anyone walking along Main Street had a pretty good view of us through the Salon's front window and the open massage room door. I decided not to mention that.

Jammie finally got ahold of herself and, wiping tears from her eyes, closed the door. Unfortunately, she closed it with me still inside the room—the last place I wanted to be after committing what could arguably be considered a sexual assault on my client.

"So sorry, Sandra. This will never happen again. Breast time is free. Next! *Next* time is free!" Horrified, I hauled ass out of the room and away from Sandra, who was hurling angry threats at me about hiring a lawyer and suing my pants off.

Laila caught my eye as I was hustling to get out of there and find my daughter. She appeared to have been laughing as hard as Jammie since she also had tears running down her face. Still, Laila had the decency to send a look of commiseration my way. "I tried to stop Kinsley. That girl is determined when she wants to be."

I grunted and shoved the front door open. Kinsley was leaning against the side of the building holding an unlit cigarette between her teeth. I stormed over, yanked the cigarette out of her mouth, threw it on the ground, and pinned her with my hardest glare. "You are in so much trouble, Kinsley Maude Day. I don't even know where to start!"

"What. Ever." She rolled her eyes and crossed her arms over her chest. "You wouldn't give me extra money this morning to see a movie after school with my friends, so what was I supposed to do? I need a ride home."

"Kinsley, I have told you so many times not to enter my massage room like that when I'm working. People are undressed and relaxed, and the last thing they want is a teenager barging in and exposing them to the entire island! And what's with the cigarette? We've discussed that already. You're too young to smoke. It's not just my rule; it's the law. Do you want to damage your lungs? Do we need to go over again all the nasty ways tobacco can destroy a person's health?"

"Oh my god, Mom. Chill out. I'm a freaking shifter. Cigarettes won't kill me."

"We don't know that!" I wanted to smack my child. I didn't believe in striking a child, but part of me, the part that was at my wit's end, was seconds away from it. "Our cottage is five minutes away—you can walk. As soon as you get home, have a snack and do your homework. If I'm not home before you finish your homework, get started on your chores."

"I am not a child!" She shoved off the wall and shouldered past me. Being a shifter, she was a lot stronger than I was, and I had to put on a brave face like it hadn't hurt. "Fine! I'll walk home! I'll probably get kidnapped by human traffickers and you'll spend the rest of your life drowning in guilt for letting it happen to me. Great job, Mom!"

I stayed where I was, fists balled up, the breath in my lungs sizzling from the anger raging through me. I counted to five. "Don't forget to take Boots for a walk!"

"What. Ever!"

I turned and watched her go. She didn't have very far to walk, but that comment about traffickers got to me. Something *could* happen. I should at least keep an eye on her while she was on Main Street. Magnolia Street had its own neighborhood watch. Her name was Elsie Smith. Since moving to Sunkissed Key six months earlier, old Mrs. Smith had called me no less than twelve times with reports on my daughter.

As soon as my child turned onto Magnolia, she shot me a nasty scowl over her shoulder, and I relaxed a bit. She just had a block and a half to walk on Magnolia before she reached the cottage we rented. She was fine. Well, she was safe as far as her walk home, anyway. *Fine* was relative.

Suddenly exhausted, both mentally and physically, I leaned against the front of Jammie's Salon and tried to focus on calming myself. Being a parent was hard. Being a single parent was even harder. My life had been challenging since the day Kinsley had come into the world. I'd had to grow up in a hurry that day. She'd been such a sweet little baby and a loving little girl, but her pleasant demeanor changed drastically once she hit puberty. She seemed to grow a little more indignant and bad tempered every day. I didn't understand why she was so angry. Ninety-nine percent of the time, she seemed angry or lashing out—usually at me.

I was stressed to the breaking point, but I couldn't afford to break. I felt as though my daughter hated me, and since the move to Sunkissed Key, I hadn't made any close friends. Isolation and loneliness probably added to the stress created by my daughter. I let out a slow breath. Feeling like a failure as a mother sucked.

Straightening my shoulders, I readjusted my ponytail and forced a professionally pleasant smile. It probably looked fake as hell, but I was trying. I strode back inside, pretending I wasn't thinking about Kinsley and all the things she might be doing at home to get back at me.

2

HARRISON

"Parker and baby Stella in room four, Doc." My nurse, Polly, tapped a file against my chest and stared up at me. At five feet, she was over a foot and a half shorter than I was, but that didn't stop the sassy older woman from bossing me around like it was her job. "They're new patients and the momma looks nervous."

I took the file and nodded at her. "Thank you, Polly."

"And take off the Dr. Grumpy mask." She wagged her finger at me and made a clucking sound of disproval before walking off. I shook my head. This morning I'd had a two-year-old nearly bite the tip of my finger off, an eight-month-old urinate on me, and a four-year-old haul off and kick me in the shin, and *I'm* grumpy. Go figure.

I rapped on the door quickly and entered. I scented rabbit shifter. Being the only pediatrician on Sunkissed Key who was also a shifter, all the shifter children on the island eventually became my patients. They almost never got sick, but they had their own individual set of needs. I heeded Polly's warning about being grumpy, plastered a smile on my face, and held out my hand to the mom, Parker Pettit. "Hello, Mrs. Pettit, I'm Dr. Daniels. It's nice to meet you."

Her eyes widened, and she clapped her hands together. "Call me Parker, and you're perfect!"

I sat on my stool and attempted to keep my smile genuine. "Excuse me?"

"I'm starting a mate-matching service. It's still in the start-up stage, but I've already made one match."

So much for a genuine smile. I attempted to divert her attention to her infant. "So, how is baby Stella doing at home? Any issues or concerns you'd like to discuss—sleeping, feeding, anything? About Stella, I mean. Anything about Stella."

"Oh, she's fine. Dr. Grabowski at the hospital in Miami examined her yesterday. She's a little bunny shifter, after all. She's thriving." Seeing my confusion, she just grinned wider. "Dr. Grabowski birthed *me*. He's great and all, but you're an actual pediatrician and much younger."

I shrugged. "Not that young, but I am a pediatrician and skilled in shifter development. And I suppose it's a bonus I'm right here on the island."

"Absolutely. When I heard about the bachelor shifter pediatrician in town, I had to come see for myself, and I'm so glad I did. The service I'm starting is called Cybermates. I'm actively recruiting subscribers, and I need more males to enroll. I signed up all my female shifter friends, acquaintances, and friends of friends. The ones who aren't mated, anyway, but it's been difficult finding enough eligible men. You are perfect—handsome, educated, employed, good with kids!"

I sat back and crossed my arms over my chest. "So, you're not here for a well-baby exam for Stella?"

"No, I am. I'll bring her to you from now on. She's good right now, though. This was more of an introductory visit. Dr. Daniels, meet Stella. Stella, meet Dr. Daniels. Okay, now that that's out of the way, back to Cybermates."

I found it odd that I was slightly intimidated by the woman. I'd never known a rabbit that came on so strong. Especially when face to face with a dominant grizzly like myself. "Um... I'm good in that regard."

"Uh-uh. Nope. You're single, right?"

7

In need of a distraction, I lifted Stella from her baby carrier and cradled her in my arms. She looked up at me with big blue eyes and grinned a toothless grin. Well, well, the baby bunny rabbit wa s not the least bit afraid of a great big grizzly, either. "I am single."

"Oh, look, she loves you!" Parker pulled out her phone and snapped a picture. "So, you're single. Any hidden psychoses or physical deformities that might be a deal breaker to a potential partner?"

"I do have one deal breaker—the fact that I'm not interested in finding a mate."

She rolled her eyes. "All of you men seem to say that. None of you are ever looking or even ready for a mate. Then, you meet her—the one—and it's a whole different can of beans. I'm here to make that happen."

This woman refused to take no for an answer. I growled under my breath and little Stella giggled. "I'm sorry, Parker. I'm truly not interested."

"I'll tell you what. I'll throw in a coupon for a free massage if you give it a two-week trial. All you have to do is fill out the application." She rifled through the diaper bag.

I just stared at her, incredulous.

"Ah, here it is. A free thirty-minute massage at Jammie's Salon. And here's the application."

I shook my head, but before I could reiterate my rejection, she was already sliding Stella out of my arms and the coupon and application into my hand.

"You won't regret it. And you can even drop the application off at Jammie's when you go for the massage. You want to give it to a blonde stylist named Laila. If you don't use that coupon, I'll find out. And I'll be back."

"Are you always this overbearing?"

"Oh yeah." She laughed. "Ask my mate."

"Look, I'm happy with my life the way it is. I'm not looking for a mate."

"I hear you. Just fill out the application for me, anyway. If you don't, Stella might need a doctor's visit every time she burps. Just to be safe."

I held up my hands. "Fine. I'll fill out the application, if you promise not to come back unless Stella *really* needs something."

With a triumphant smirk, Parker tapped the coupon in my hand. "You won't regret it. And enjoy your massage. You won't regret that, either." At that, she waved Stella's chubby little hand at me and strutted victoriously out of the room, leaving me more than a little baffled and confused about what had just transpired.

I stayed in the room for a few more seconds, staring at the wall and considering the fact that a bunny rabbit shifter had just bullied me into signing up for an online mate-matching service. Rubbing my forehead where a headache was beginning to form, I left the room in search of Polly. She was leaning against the reception desk, chatting with Parker.

"Well, well, well, if it isn't Casanova." Polly threw her head back and chuckled, knowing good and well that I did not want a mate. A tiger shifter herself, she'd been with her mate for forty years and made a frequent hobby out of teasing me about how much I enjoyed the uncomplicated life of a bachelor.

"Hardly."

Parker grinned and winked at me. "We'll see about that."

I snarled and peeked into the reception area. There were a few patients waiting. Billy Hill was back. Poor kid. His high-strung mother was convinced there was something wrong with him because of his occasional bedwetting.

Even Billy's mom was a welcome distraction from Polly and Parker joining forces. I glanced again at the two women and backed away. "Billy? You want to come on back, buddy?"

The kid rose with all the pep and vigor of Eeyore, the children's character from Winnie-the-Pooh. With head low and eyes on the floor, he lumbered toward me. His mom was wringing her hands, a magazine in the crook of her arm, as she followed Billy. Her giant purse dragged along the ground when she stooped over to hurriedly shove her magazine back in the rack. "Wait on me, Billy."

Billy wasn't waiting. He stepped up his pace, clearly trying to get as much distance between him and his mother as possible. Grumbling as he walked past, he made a beeline for the room that Parker and Stella had just vacated without waiting for me to give him instructions.

"Don't forget to drop off the paperwork to Laila!" Parker called out as she held open the door of the clinic on her way out. "And get that massage. I didn't want to say anything, but you look a little tense, Doc."

I turned and hurried after Billy, suddenly realizing I knew exactly how the kid felt.

3

FERN

"Do not drop me off in front of the school, Mom. I mean it." Kinsley slid down in her seat and groaned. "I do not want to be seen in this ghetto-mobile. Oh my god, I'm going to die of cringe."

I stepped on the brakes of my minivan a little too firmly, and the car behind me on Main Street tapped their horn. "Watch your mouth. And there's nothing wrong with this van, Kinsley. There was nothing wrong with it when I used it to drop you off at your last school."

"Oh my god, Mom! Everyone is going to see me! You're making a huge scene!"

I stared over at my daughter and drew in a deep breath. "Kinsley, it's too early in the morning for your attitude. We're in front of the school, there's a line of cars behind me, and you need to get out. Please. Just get out of the vehicle."

"No! No freaking way. Pull around." Ducking even lower, Kinsley glowered at me. "Are you kidding me? Do you see those Beamers and Escalades? And you're really dropping me off in the ghetto-mobile? Do you even know how much shit I'm gonna get? This is just great. The entire school gets a front-row ticket to watch my popularity take a nose dive."

Taken aback by her cruel attack on me and my finances, I stared at her for a second, speechless. Another horn—this one from a Hummer behind us—brought me back to reality. My anger boiled over and I saw red. "Let me tell you something…"

But, what? What was I going to say? I really want to go off on her, tell her how much of a struggle it was for me to keep a roof over our heads and all the bills paid, and do it all by myself. I wanted to point out that although they may not be the top of the line, her clothes and shoes were trendy, and she had her own cellphone. And that I'd had to work extra hours to provide her with those luxuries. I knew better, though. Been there, tried that. No matter how many times I explained, she never understood.

Instead, I shifted hard into park, threw my door open, stomped around to the passenger door of the minivan, jerked that open, and gestured for her to get out. Then, I used words she *would* understand. Loudly. "Out! Let's go sugar booger, apple dumplin', puddin' pie. I have to get the ghetto-mobile back to the run-down trailer park, but we can discuss this later over an ice-cold glass of get over yourself."

"Ugh! I hate you!" She jumped out of the minivan and kept her head down as she raced into the school, almost at an all-out run.

"Smooches!" I shouted after her.

The Hummer honked again, and I smiled politely while grinding my teeth so hard, my jaw hurt. I really had to fight to keep myself from flipping them the bird. "I'm going!"

Getting back in my *ghetto-mobile*, I forced myself to drive carefully and slowly out of the lot, despite wanting to burn rubber. It was never-ending with her. There was always something wrong, something awful, or something embarrassing that I was doing to wreck Kinsley's life. My anger still sizzled under the surface, but guilt was slowly replacing it. I hated losing my temper with her, but I was only human for Christ's sake, and she knew how to push every single one of my buttons. I hadn't even realized I had some of the buttons she found to push.

By the time I drove the short distance to work at Jammie's Salon, my anger and guilt had me on the verge of tears. The morning had been an overwhelming shit show. Boots, our new puppy, had pooped on the kitchen floor as soon as Kinsley let him out of his crate in the morning. I told her to take him right from the crate to the backyard, but she didn't listen. Then, and I'm not really sure how, his awkward puppy paws ran straight through the poop and slipped and slid around before he raced through the house making a game of me chasing him. Smeared poo everywhere.　•

Of course, Kinsley wouldn't touch the dog poop with a ten-foot pooper scooper. Fresh out of the shower and before my first cup of coffee, I bathed Boots, washed the kitchen floor, scrubbed the poop spots out of the carpet, and ended up having to shower again. As an added bonus, I got to be the target for a mouthy teen's cutting insults. Plus, I was awarded the grand prize of stress, frustration, and feelings of parental inadequacy—all before eight in the morning. Lucky me. Still never got that first cup of coffee, either.

My neck and shoulders were so tight that I was already picturing the ice pack in the fridge at work draped across them. When I entered the salon, though, Laila and her friend Parker were standing together in the small back corner that served as a breakroom.

I'd met Parker a couple of times and her sweet little baby girl, Stella. She was always friendly, but my current mood was in the dumps, so I wanted to avoid conversation. I wouldn't be surprised if my own personal storm cloud was hanging over my head following me wherever I went. I just wanted to slip into my room and have a couple of minutes alone to regroup.

No such luck. Laila spotted me. "Hey! We were just talking about you!"

I told my face to smile, but when nothing happened, Laila's expression turned to one of concern. Seeing her concern, I burst into tears. Fat, ugly tears that I knew were ruining my mascara and leaving streaks in the bronzer I'd brushed over my cheeks to look like I wasn't a newcomer to the island. I'm sure I looked stupid, but damn if the tears didn't make me feel better.

"Oh, Fern!" Laila hurried to my side and wrapped her arm around my shoulders while Parker grabbed tissues and lightly dabbed at my face. "What's going on?"

Parker swallowed so loudly that it was audible in the small kitchenette. "Oh no. I'm going to cry, too. Crap."

I laughed through my tears and patted her on the arm. "Don't cry. I'm done. It was just a much-needed momentary stress reliever. "

Laila raised a brow. "What the hell, Parker? Why are you crying?"

"Since the baby, I can't help it. It just keeps happening." She waved a tissue at me. "Ignore me. Tell us what's wrong. Whose ass do we need to kick?"

"Are you opposed to throttling teenagers?"

Parker shook her head while Laila rolled her eyes and squeezed my shoulder. "Kinsley? She's a tough one alright. What happened?"

"Apparently, my minivan is a complete embarrassment, and I'm a woefully inadequate joke." I sniffled and took a tissue to blow my nose. "And our puppy pooped all over the kitchen floor this morning because she let him out of his crate and didn't take him right outside. No one ever warned me that my sweet little angel would grow into a vicious monster."

"I don't want to picture Stella as a moody teenager. I like my little cherub so much right now." Parker cried harder and leaned against the kitchen counter. "Oh god. She's going to grow up too fast and she's going to go through the bratty stage and think her parents are old, stupid, and out of touch, isn't she?"

Laila held up her hands and groaned. "Both of you, knock it off. Stella is perfect, and Kinsley's going through a phase. We all went through it. It won't last forever."

I huffed. "I don't know about that. She hates me. It's not just me. She hates everything."

"How old is she?" Parker's eyes had dried and she leaned in.

"Fifteen."

"Fifteen! No way. What, were you five when you had her?" She leaned in closer and stared at the skin around my eyes looking for wrinkles.

"I was fifteen."

Laila slapped her friend's arm and winced. "Sorry. Parker didn't mean to be so nosy."

I waved them off. "No, it's fine. It happened. It's a part of me. No big deal."

"Is she…" Parker wrinkled her nose and looked up, like she was trying to spot the words in the air.

Laila nodded, reading her mind. "She's a shifter. Wolf."

"But, you're not."

I shook my head. "Nope."

"You should take her to see Dr. Daniels. He's a pediatrician. He sees shifter kids on the island up until age eighteen, sometimes longer. I just took Stella to his office yesterday."

I made a face. "I don't think she's ill. Just a moody, sullen smart-ass. She's on birth control, for obvious reasons, so she'll have to see him eventually, but I think she's okay right now."

"He could talk to you about the hormone changes she's going through right now. It might help. Plus, he's hot and single."

"You better hope Maxim doesn't hear you say that."

Parker stared at me with an interested look on her face. "Maxim is *super* hot. And taken. I also gave Dr. Daniels one of those coupons for a free massage, the ones that you were giving out when you first started working here. I still had mine, so I used it as an incentive to get him to fill out the paperwork for Cybermates. I told him he could drop it off here, but if he doesn't, he's getting another visit from me."

I shrugged. "I don't know. With Kinsley, everything's a struggle. Dragging her to the doctor, well, I don't know if I'm ready for that fight yet." I sighed. "You really think it'll help?"

"Yes, I do. You won't regret it. A fifteen-year-old shifter has more hormones raging through her body than a fifteen-year-old human. It's not just her human side that's undergoing an incredible transformation. There's an animal in there, too, that's changing and growing. All those hormones can make a person crazy—especially a female. We get hit harder, for some reason. Doesn't seem fair. Half of her fury is probably just hormones right now. Dr. Daniels could talk you through what to do."

"I'll give it a try. Although, I don't see how he can help...unless his answer is duct taping her mouth."

4

HARRISON

"Sara's throat looks great. How's she been with the recovery?" I sat on my stool across from little Sara Brooks and her mother, Jeanie.

"Wonderful. You did such a great job, Dr. Daniels." Jeanie Douglas ran her hand up and down my arm affectionately as she spoke. Was the woman actually batting her lashes?

I shifted slightly away from her and forced a smile. "All I did was recommend she have her tonsils removed. Dr. Dean did all the hard work."

"I got to eat ice cream all week long." Sara wiggled on the exam table and stared at the basket of toys in the corner of the room.

"That sounds like—" Muffled shouts drifted in from somewhere on the other side of the closed exam room door. Something was going on in the clinic. I glanced back at the door and frowned. It was solid wood. My shifter hearing was good, but someone was *really* shouting up a storm out there. "Excuse me."

I left Jeanie and Sara in the exam room and slipped away to find the source of the ruckus. I found it. A girl, midteens, red-faced, arms waving, was hollering hysterically at a woman whose back was to me. I sniffed the air. The girl was a shifter. A wolf. And the woman...

"I'm not a child! I can't believe you brought me here! You tricked me! You're such a liar!"

Polly stood by the pair, trying to de-escalate the situation. "Honey, calm down. Your mother is concerned about you, is all. You shouldn't speak to her that way."

"Mind your own business, old lady!"

"Kinsley! Watch your mouth! There are children here and you're setting a bad example." The woman, whom I assumed was the mom, ran her hands through her hair and sighed. "Can we please just sit and discuss this quietly?"

"I'm leaving! You can't make me stay here."

I growled low in my throat, making my presence known. "Both of you, sit down!" The bellowing command that emerged from my chest was more of a growly roar, not quite human.

The woman jumped and spun around to face me, her eyes wide. The startled sound she made as her hand flew to her chest made me instantly regret scaring her.

"Thank god, Doctor. Kinsley here thinks she's too old for a pediatrician. Want to enlighten her?" Polly walked away, her hands thrown in the air in frustration.

The girl, Polly, and everything around me faded away as I focused on the mom. The sweet scent of wild honey filled my nostrils, and my entire body buzzed like I was touching an electric fence. *Mate.*

My bear urged me to grab her, take her, toss her over my shoulder, and claim her. Fortunately, although my body leaned toward her, I managed to override the animal instinct and keep my feet firmly planted where they were.

I had to force my eyes away from the—human?—woman in front of me to stare down at the angry little wolf shifter. She was still standing, scowling at me with her arms crossed angrily over her chest. Worse, she was snarling at her mother with every other glance. "Sit down and be quiet."

"You can't talk to me like that!" Rage filled her young eyes—eyes, I noticed, that were a shade darker than her mother's lovely emerald ones. "Mom, tell him he can't talk to me like that."

Her mom blinked and turned to her daughter before stealing another glance back at me. "He most certainly can. This is his clinic and you're out-of-control behavior warrants it, Kinsley."

Clearly irate and indignant, I witnessed her wolf flash into her eyes again and again. She seemed to be struggling with her animal. Kinsley glared but sat heavily in one of the waiting room chairs. "What. Ever."

Her mom released a tired breath and also sat—three chairs down from the angry teen. The woman's cheeks were bright red and, as I watched, the color spread down her neck and across her chest. When it disappeared into the modest neckline of her shirt, I found myself leaning forward, wanting to see how far that blush went.

"Sorry, everyone." She looked tired and defeated.

"Don't apologize for me. I didn't do anything wrong. You're the one who dragged me to a stupid little kid doctor. This is humiliating."

I growled at the teen, louder than I meant to. When she froze, I forced myself to step back and regain my composure. "No more fighting in my reception area. I'll be with you both soon. And you, young lady, don't move from that chair until I return. Got it?"

The girl shot me the stink-eye, but I was pretty sure I'd sufficiently intimidated her. I left them there, the daughter still fuming and the mother near tears. Instead of going back into the exam room with Sara and Jeanie, I stepped into my office and closed the door. Turning, I braced my arms against the solid-wood door, taking a moment to compose myself and suck in a much-needed lungful of air.

"Dr. Daniels?" Polly tapped her knuckles on the door. "Sara Douglas is still waiting in exam room two to finish up with you, and then you've got three other appointments ahead of Kinsley Day. This is not a good time for a break."

I shoved my hands through my hair and tugged at it. "Polly, I need a minute."

I needed more than a minute. I'd just been hit with the equivalent of a sledgehammer to the chest. That woman… That *human*… I sucked in another breath and forced myself to blow it out slowly. She was mine. She was the one—my mate.

"Sonofabitch."

"Excuse me?" Polly was right next to the door, eavesdropping.

"Never mind, Polly. Go away."

"Don't play Dr. Grumpy with me, mister."

I swore again and straightened. My mate had just walked into my office with her angry little wolf-child. My *mate*. How she'd found my clinic, I didn't know. The whole thing was scarcely believable.

"You're getting my clinic backed up."

I was going to strangle Polly. I jerked open the door and frowned at her. "Woman, I am having a personal crisis right now. Do you mind?"

She rolled her eyes. "Yes, I mind. I'd like to get home at a decent hour tonight, so I suggest you get over your, ahem, *personal crisis*, ASAP and resume doctoring. Your scheduled appointments await."

I didn't like the way she said personal crisis, as though it was something trite and trivial. Growling loudly enough to rattle the walls, I stomped back into exam room two with Sara and Jeanie Douglas, slamming the door harder than I'd meant to. When Sara jumped, I winced, instantly remorseful.

"I apologize." *My mate is in the waiting room, and my destiny beckons.* I bent the metal of my stethoscope. "Sorry. Um, where were we?"

Jeanie's flirty looks recommenced. When she reached out to touch my arm, I moved, deftly avoiding her reach. "I think we're all set here. Sara looks great. She's healing nicely."

Jeanie frowned, lifting her purse onto her shoulder as Sara hopped off the exam table and smiled at me. She held out her hand and wagged her eyebrows. I pulled a sucker from my pocket and plopped it into her hand, eliciting a giggle. When Jeanie Douglas opened her mouth to say something, I quickly cut her off at the pass.

"No need for a follow up unless she suddenly develops pain or a fever. That's doubtful, though. Dr. Dean took good care of you." I had already scooted past them and was headed to my office. "I'll see you next year, young lady, for your annual checkup."

A few minutes later, Polly popped her head in my office door. "Another break, huh? The life of leisure sure must be nice."

"Polly, don't start. I'm in no mood." I shook my head and groaned. "I am your boss, you know. You could pretend to be at least mildly intimidated by me. I do have the authority to fire you."

"Hmph!" she scoffed, haughtily. "Just try and run this place without me, *boss*."

I bit my lip to hide a grin. "I wouldn't dare."

5

FERN

I sat as still as possible, hoping I wasn't giving away the thoughts and feelings that were creating swirls of turmoil on my insides. My cheeks were on fire. I silently hoped everyone around me assumed it was because my daughter was out of control. It wasn't.

I leaned forward so I could see down the hallway where the doctor had just disappeared. A quick glance, that was all, then eyes back on my feet. Parker had not done him justice. *Hot* was not nearly descriptive enough for the man who'd come out of the back of the clinic and startled me stupid. I'd never once considered that love at first sight was actually a thing. I still didn't. I was a realist. Lust at first sight, however…

Dr. Daniels probably had a line of mothers wrapped around the block. Glancing around the room, I noticed that the other moms were dressed to the nines. No one was in anything less than their Sunday best, fully made up, not a hair out of place. When my gaze scanned to a busty woman in the corner, I did a double-take. Who the heck dressed in stilettos and a teensy black cocktail dress to take their kid to the doctor's office? I looked down at my own attire. I'd taken the morning off work, so my hair was piled haphazardly atop my head in a messy bun and, like most days, I hadn't bothered applying makeup. I was wearing old jeans, Converse, and a T-shirt that said, "I got it all together—but I forgot where I put it."

Shit, maybe Kinsley was right. I *was* an embarrassment. I glanced over at my daughter and felt a pang of grief. I wanted to be able to ask her how I looked, or even if I had body odor, because I wasn't sure whether I'd remembered deodorant this morning. Asking my daughter those questions, though, would result in my self-esteem being ripped to shreds. I'd learned the hard way that exposing my vulnerabilities to my teenage daughter was a bad idea. Kinsley could be brutal when given the opportunity.

I ran my hand down my T-shirt and tugged at the hem to smooth it.

"Kinsley? Come on back." The sweet older nurse motioned for us to follow her, her wary gaze pinned to my problem child. "I'll get you set up in exam room one, and Dr. Daniels will be with you shortly."

I swallowed down the inappropriate attraction I was feeling toward the handsome doctor and met Kinsley's angry gaze. When I stood, Kinsley growled at me. "You do not need to come."

"Well, I am anyway." I sent an apologetic look to the nurse. "Thank you for being patient with us. I'm really sorry."

"Oh, honey, you're fine." She led us to a room in the back, a strategic move, I was sure, and patted my shoulder after Kinsley went in. "Hang in there, Momma."

I laughed and nodded. "I'm hanging. And the noose is tightening."

"Well, my name is Polly. Y'all call me if you need anything." She squeezed my arm and left us in the closed room together.

The room was way too small to hold both me and my raging daughter. Normally, an entire house wasn't big enough. Kinsley sat in the only chair in the room, wearing an angry scowl and staring through me.

Deciding that for me to sit on an exam table in a pediatrician's office was strange, I stood bracing myself against the wall. I was worn out. As usual, instead of my morning off being peaceful and restorative, I was wound tighter than a two-dollar watch. On top of that, I was weirdly attracted to a doctor I'd only seen for all of two minutes while he scolded my child. I thought about the way the mothers out in the waiting room were dressed, quite obviously attempting to catch the eye of the handsome, single doctor, and said a silent prayer. *Lord, don't let me sink that low. Or at least don't let me be so obvious about it.*

Leaning against the wall by the window, I stared out at the partial view of the gulf. I hadn't been swimming yet. We'd been on the island for six months and I still hadn't sunk a single toe in sand or saltwater. My life was too hectic to find any me-time or to indulge in enjoyable pastimes. Lately, my daughter was so full of defiance and what seemed to be outright anger that I spent a lot of time diffusing her potential detonations or cleaning up post explosion. When I wasn't fighting with her, enforcing her punishment, or walking on eggshells, I was working a job to keep our little family of two afloat. It was a vicious cycle and I needed a break.

I wasn't under any delusions that Dr. Daniels was going to be the answer to my prayers. How was a pediatrician supposed to solve our problems? But, since I had no other avenues to turn to, there I was, wringing my hands while waiting for the doctor. I wasn't hopeful, but I was desperate. I didn't know how much longer I could battle with Kinsley without having some sort of breakdown myself.

A quick tap on the door made me jump, then the doctor stepped into the room. If it'd felt small and cramped before, it became suffo-cating and minuscule once he stepped in. He was huge, probably about six and a half feet tall with broad shoulders. Imposing as hell, especially when those dark eyes fell on me.

I straightened. My heart instantly went into overdrive, pumping too hard and too fast. My stomach tightened, and I could feel a blush creep up my cheeks. I stroked a palm over my hair as though that might magically transform my sloppy up-do into a sleek, sophisti-cated style.

"Um… Hello. I'm Fern Day. This is my daughter, Kinsley." I sounded strange and had an urge to crawl under the exam table. "I want to thank you for fitting us in today."

Kinsley groaned. "He knows who we are, Mom. He has the file."

Dr. Daniels looked over at Kinsley and frowned. "Is there something wrong with your legs?"

"No."

"Then you should hop up on the exam table and give your mother the chair." There was a raspy growl to his deep voice, grit and gravel that made it sound like he didn't use it much although, given his profession, that couldn't be true.

Kinsley paused a beat and I held my breath not knowing what her reaction was going to be. Then, she sighed and did as he'd suggested. She crossed her arms over her chest and sent a scathing look my way. "I don't even know why I'm here. There is nothing wrong with me."

Still standing, I found myself wrapping my arms around my stomach, suddenly more self-conscious about my failures as a parent than my appearance. "One of my coworkers is a shifter and she mentioned you might be able to help. My daughter and I... We're having a lot of issues lately."

Dr. Daniels motioned toward the chair and waited until I perched on the edge—significantly closer to him than when I was standing—before he spoke. "Kinsley's a wolf shifter. Since you're not, she obviously inherited it from her father. Has he discussed with you what it's like for a wolf shifter to go through puberty?"

"Oh gawd, kill me now. *Puberty*? I'm fifteen, not twelve." Kinsley snarled. "Plus, my dad didn't stick around. He couldn't handle her shit, either."

My jaw dropped and my back stiffened as pain lanced through me. I was so hurt by her words, I wanted to toss my child out the window. I'd open it first, of course. And although we were on the ground floor, it still might feel really good to give her a good toss.

Dr. Daniels growled deep in his chest and spoke before I could figure out how to respond to Kinsley's rudeness. "Okay, Kinsley. I get it. You're angry. There are a lot of changes and transformations happening in your body right now, and your emotions are all over the place, which makes everything worse. Being a teenager and a shifter is hard, but that's no excuse for taking it out on your mom. That won't make anything better for you. I suggest you drop the attitude and talk about it. As a shifter who went through some teenage angst myself, I think I can offer you some helpful advice or at least be a sounding board. Let's talk."

Kinsley sat forward. "You're a shifter?"

"I am. And if you turn your focus from honing that ill temper of yours to something productive like honing your shifter senses, you'd know that." He turned to me. "Are you alright?"

I sat back in the chair and nodded. My eyes burned and there was a lump in my throat. I wasn't sure if it was because of the kindness and concern in Dr. Daniel's eyes when he looked at me or because of the way my daughter responded to his openness and honesty. I bit my lip and turned my face to the window. I wasn't going to cry. I wasn't. But I was starting to hope—for the first time in a long time. Maybe he *could* help Kinsley. Maybe Dr. Harrison Daniels was exactly what we needed.

6

HARRISON

I had a strong urge to order the young wolf shifter to a time-out corner until she learned to show some respect for her mother. My bear was fuming, yet it was a controlled fury. The little wolf's scent left no doubt she was our mate's progeny. Hidden beneath the raging adolescent hormones and lupine fur, she carried the subtle and slightly altered scent of her mother. Already, my sworn-to-single-hood bear fully accepted the inevitable changes about to take place in our life. He liked being in a small exam room with his mate and her child as much as I did. The girl was the offspring of our mate, therefore ours by default. Her bad attitude and all.

I wasn't feeling as compassionate toward the smart-mouthed hell-raiser as my bear. Not when she was snapping vicious retorts at her mom every chance she got. Each breath seemed to be another blatant insult, another pointed jab meant to inflict pain. It was all I could do to keep myself from snapping at her in defense. Especially after witnessing the tears pool in my mate's eyes.

"I see you're on birth control pills, so I imagine your mother gave you *the talk* about the changes taking place with your body." Without waiting for one of her snarky comebacks, I pushed forward. "But with shifters, the changes are a little different and a lot more intense. Do you have any shifter friends?"

Kinsley shrugged. "I never asked."

I smiled at Kinsley and was thrilled to watch some of her anger melt away. "Once you sharpen your sense of smell, you won't need to ask. You'll be able to tell instantly. As soon as I entered the reception area out front, I knew you were a wolf shifter and your mother was fully human.

"So, the short and not-as-awkward version of *the talk* for shifters is that you're going to have twice as many hormones going twice as crazy. Your emotions are going to be doubly difficult to deal with. There will be frustration, unexplained anger, and other...more embarrassing feelings that we won't discuss here unless you want to, and so much hunger. You can expect to be 'hangry' pretty much nonstop."

"I'm always starving, but I try not to eat because I don't want to get fat."

"You won't. Your metabolism is soaring. You *need* to eat a lot of food. Especially when you shift."

"I had no idea..." Fern covered her mouth with her hand and leaned forward in the chair. "I'm so sorry, Kinsley. I... I should've asked someone, or researched it somehow, someway. I never dreamed adolescence was different for a shifter."

I shook my head and turned to face her. It was hard being so close to her, wanting to offer comfort, yet not daring to touch her. Not yet. "There was no way you could've known. And while there is a valid explanation for her mood swings as well as her frustration and anger, none of that is an excuse for her rude attitude to you."

Kinsley grunted. "I'm not rude."

"I seem to remember a fifteen-year-old screaming at her mother in the reception area not twenty minutes ago."

"It's fine. I mean, it's not *fine*, but I can handle it. Right now, I just want to learn. What else don't I know about my daughter that I should? Tell me everything. What should I be doing? How can I help her?" Leaning forward again, Fern cast pleading eyes to mine. "And shifting? How does she shift? I can't believe I've never thought to search out someone to ask about it. I feel like such an idiot."

"That's what I've been saying all along."

Growling at the girl, I narrowed my eyes at her. "What did I say, Miss Rude 'Tude?"

"Ugh! Mom, are you going to do anything about him calling me lame names?"

Fern rolled her eyes. "Honestly, it's less name-calling and more fact, Kinsley. Your attitude is incredibly rude."

I couldn't help but laugh. "Okay, okay. I won't call you Miss Rude 'Tude if you start treating your mom more kindly and with more respect. I'd say, despite your complaints, that she's a pretty great mom. Not everyone has a mother who's willing to take the verbal abuse you dole out and still make a herculean effort to do whatever she can to help her daughter."

"What. Ever. She's nothing like me and she doesn't know the first thing about me. She's so great, but she doesn't even know I've already shifted."

The sharp intake of breath was the only telltale sign of the hurt I sensed from my mate. Her face was carefully neutral, but I sensed that composed veneer was so brittle, a gentle breeze could've shattered it.

"Did you tell her you've shifted?" When the girl shook her head no, I nodded. "So, you think being a great mom means being a mind reader?"

"What. Ever. Can you just teach me about using my senses, or whatever the other shifters know, and let me go home?"

I glanced over at Fern and quickly decided that I had to get her to return to the clinic. It was clear that this wasn't the appropriate time for me to lay the big news on her that we were mates. She was in no shape emotionally for me to drop that bomb right here and now, but she'd be ready eventually. She needed time—I needed her to come back. "We can go over some stuff today, sure. It won't be hard, especially if you're already shifting without any problems. You aren't having any problems shifting, are you?"

Kinsley shook her head. "I'm great at it."

"I'm sure you are. So, let's work on a few things today, and then we'll set up an appointment for you and your mom to return. We'll do more work then."

As Fern met my eyes, I studied her reaction closely. Did she know that having them return was as much about me wanting to see her again as it was about her daughter? If so, she showed no signs. She seemed entirely focused on her daughter and getting her the aid she needed. "We'll come back as often it takes."

"Ugh. Come on, can't you just show me everything? I don't want my friends to see me coming out of the Children's Clinic."

"Nope." I winked at Fern and loved the fact that her intriguing blush returned, traveling down her neck and chest. Grinning like a clown from her response, I turned back to my patient and began the first lesson. It was simple stuff that I went over with all of my shifter patients. Usually, their parents had already informed them of everything, but Kinsley was a unique case. Still, she was a bright kid and caught on quickly.

All the while, her mother sat on the edge of her seat, literally, watching and listening intently. There were moments when I was fairly certain she was feeling a strong attraction to me, but those moments were few and far between. When she wasn't reacting to the fact that we were caught in the midst of a strong, primal mating desire, she barely registered I was even there. That was because she was watching her daughter so intently. She was clearly a good mother who was just in over her head. She was eager to learn, though. She hung on every word I said, and I caught her lips moving every so often, repeating the words I said back to herself.

After going over some basics, I decided to end the day's session. Kinsley seemed ready to run out, maybe hoping to practice what she learned, probably wanting to find a back door to avoid any of her friends seeing her. I smiled down at Fern, willing her to say something, give me a sign that she wanted to see me again—as a man, not as her daughter's doctor. It was incredibly obvious to me that we were mates, but I wasn't sure what that felt like for a human. Did she have any clue that this wasn't a normal attraction? That it was something far more profound?

When she dodged my gaze and hurried out after her child, I got the impression that she didn't. I followed them, watching as she stopped to talk to Polly.

"I guess Kinsley will need another appointment. Whenever is good for Dr. Daniels is okay with me."

"Anytime. Anytime is good for me. Anytime at all."

Fern looked back at me with her bottom lip held between her teeth. Then the most mesmerizing smile played across her face, freeing that lip. I inhaled sharply and she quickly looked away. Maybe she did have a clue.

The irony of the situation was not lost on me. I'd just made it clear to Parker that I didn't want a mate. And I hadn't. I'd held tightly to my convictions that I wasn't looking for a mate and that I was happy with bachelorhood. A day later, Fern walked into my clinic and effortlessly annihilated every bit of those convictions. Now I was hoping I wouldn't have to live alone in my house for much longer.

Even my sworn-to-singlehood bear was embracing the idea of mating with open arms. How could he not? Fern was stunning, she was selfless, and she was a wonderful mother. No matter what her daughter said, Fern Day loved every inch of that bratty little hellion. I rubbed my face and swore under my breath. That bratty little hellion, I realized, was about to become a full-time part of my life, too.

My life had just become much more complicated.

7

FERN

"Someone is on the phone with one of those free-massage coupons. Can they get in today?" Jammie held the phone to her chest and blew a huge bubble with her chewing gum before letting it pop and sucking it back in. The hot-pink gum matched her hot-pink hair perfectly.

I nodded, eager to book more clients. *Anything* to get my mind off the handsome doctor we'd seen the day before. My thoughts hadn't strayed far from the man, not even when Kinsley shocked the hell out of me by shifting in the kitchen. As if that wasn't bad enough, she nipped my finger when I tried to pet her. "I'm free right now, actually, if they can get here in the next half hour."

"How 'bout right now?" She paused, listened, and then laughed. "Girlfriend, yes. You get over here, too. I know you'd look great with some color on you."

I did a once-over of my already spotless massage room before dimming the lights and lighting an unscented candle. I tried to make the room as relaxing as possible for my clients. I'd just turned on the sound machine that blocked ambient noise from the salon when Jammie finished up her call.

"He'll be here in five minutes. He just works down the street." She winked. "He's a looker, too."

I came back out into the salon and leaned against Laila's station. The youngest stylist, October, was out sick, and Parker was seated in October's chair holding baby Stella close to her chest. "Thanks for sending me to Dr. Daniels. I think he's going to help tremendously with Kinsley."

"Oh, isn't he drop-dead gorgeous?" Parker fanned herself with a People magazine. "I mean, not as hot as my Maxim, but still."

I laughed awkwardly and tucked my hair behind my ears. "Sure."

Laila raised her eyebrows without looking away from her client's bangs. "Sure?"

"You're talking about Dr. Daniels the pediatrician?" The woman in her chair, whom I didn't recognize, snorted. "I've been taking my son, Henry, to him since he first opened the doors of his clinic. Henry thinks he's too old for a pediatrician now, but I'm not giving up my chances to ogle Harrison Daniels."

"Henry is twenty-three, Mary."

Parker burst into a fit of giggles that had Stella whimpering and wagging her chubby little arms. "Oh, baby, I'm sorry. Come on, don't cry."

Laila dropped her scissors and immediately took Stella into her arms. "There's my little godbaby. Are you fussy today? Come to Auntie Laila. Come on, sweetie pie."

A funny feeling came over me just as the door opened. I stared at my feet trying to figure out why my stomach had just done a flip and why my arms were suddenly covered in goose bumps. When I looked up, I found Dr. Daniels standing in front of me, staring intently. I froze, pinned in place by the look on his face. I was trying to wrap my mind around the intensity in his gaze when the large man licked his lips and stepped toward me.

Parker clapped her hands in front of my face, startling me out of my daze, and I jumped. Then she addressed Dr. Daniels. "You came!"

He glanced briefly at her and then resumed staring at me. He acted like he didn't want to look away at all. "I couldn't resist a massage."

"Dr. Daniels is going to be my newest addition to the Cybermates site. Did you bring the paperwork with you?"

"No."

Everyone in the shop seemed to have stopped what they were doing to watch the man with curiosity. We occasionally got older male clients at the salon, mostly those who were trying to hook up with Jammie, Kitty, or Margie, but it was rare to get younger ones. It was almost unheard of to get young, hot, and single ones.

"That's okay. I've made sure applications were available at several of the local business establishments here on Sunkissed Key. Laila, do you have a spare Cybermates application?"

I was too transfixed by Dr. Daniels to decipher what Parker was saying. My brain was trying to grasp why he was here.

"Um, sure. I have one right here." Laila moved to grab something from a shelf at her station, but Dr. Daniels cleared his throat and stopped her.

"No." The word was a rough growl. He cleared his throat and tried again. "I mean, I'm not filling out the form. I don't need to."

Parker grunted. "Why not? You have to, Harrison. You accepted the free-massage coupon. Those were the terms."

I caught the final words and panic hit me hard. *Massage?* He was the client coming in to redeem the free-massage coupon? I couldn't give him a massage! I wouldn't dare touch him. I couldn't trust myself.

"I have no need of your services, Parker." He looked back at me and smiled. "Polly said you were ready for me?"

Parker opened her mouth to argue, but Laila elbowed her. "He doesn't need your services, duh. Look at him."

Parker clamped her lips shut and looked from Dr. Daniels to me and back to Dr. Daniels. "Wait…"

"That's right." Dr. Daniels nodded, and I was still lost.

I tore my gaze from the doctor and watched Laila and Parker elbow each other a few more times before giggling hysterically. I didn't have a clue what was happening, but I knew I couldn't massage Dr. Harrison Daniels. I couldn't do it. My brain was acting as badly as my dramatic teenage daughter. It was threatening to shut itself down if I had to massage the man.

My body didn't get the memo my brain was putting out, though. I felt myself moving toward my room in the back and motioning for him to follow. The entire salon was dead silent, and all of them were watching. I wanted to scream at them to turn the hell around, go about their business, act normal, but I was the farthest thing from normal myself at that moment.

Dr. Daniels crossed the salon, and in two long strides, he was next to me. The radiant heat from his large body enveloped me, making my brain fuzzier. He looked down and smiled again. "When Polly insisted I redeem the coupon, I didn't know you'd be the masseuse. This is a pleasant surprise. *Very* pleasant."

Parker scrunched her face up in an exaggerated wink. "I'm just going to turn the radio up. For the next hour, or so. You kids get as loud as you want." She gave Dr. Daniels two thumbs-up.

Horrified, I felt my face turn beet red. I was going to murder that woman. How should I explain her to Dr. Daniels? I mean, should I apologize for my perverted friend, who openly implied that he and I were about to do the naughty-naughty in the back while business went on as usual in the front? It was then that I realized that I hadn't said a word to him yet. The entire time he'd been in the salon, I hadn't uttered one word. Oh god, I was being so fucking weird!

8

FERN

"The weather is lovely today, isn't it?" Turning my back to Dr. Daniels, I closed my eyes and let a silent scream of mortification echo through my brain. *The weather is lovely?* What was I even saying? Why was I talking about the weather? I was such a complete freak!

He replied by grunting softly, effectively killing that line of conversation. He stood waiting. Even with my back turned to him, I could feel him.

I put on a blank expression and gathered every ounce of my self-control in an attempt to at least appear to be professional. I sidestepped him and pushed the door closed. "You can undress behind the screen. For the massage! Just for massage. I mean, you can undress for any reason you want. I'm not the boss of you."

I should probably just tie a cinderblock around my ankles and take a long walk off a short pier. Why couldn't I stop acting so strangely? *Someone, please, put me out of my misery.*

Dr. Daniels stepped behind the curtain, thankfully, giving me a break from having to further embarrass myself. The sounds of his clothing being draped over the chair behind the screen were like fireworks going off in the small room. I thought I heard him removing his shoes and socks, then a shirt, pants... He stopped.

"Um, you can leave your underwear on. And there are towels to wrap around yourself on the shelf to your left."

"Not wearing underwear."

I gulped audibly, nodded, nodded again, and kept nodding, until I realized that I needed to speak again. The man made basic functioning hard. "Commando. That's...that's...yeah...fine. Just wrap the towel around your waist and lie face down on the table out here."

"Are you alright?"

Now there was a question. Was I alright? No, probably not. "Yeah, sure. I'm fine. I'm just fine. I've just never massaged...uh...one of Kinsley's doctors before. It's a little weird. A bit of a mental hurdle, is all. But I'm perfectly fine."

I heard him groan as he settled on the massage table.

"Are *you* okay? Is there anything hurting?" Turning to face him, I noticed him discreetly adjusting himself before settling back on the table face down with his arms on the armrests.

He chuckled darkly. "I'm okay. It's an unusual situation for me, too. I'm looking forward to it, though."

My laugh was high pitched and stilted—one of the oddest sounds I've ever made. I really needed to get myself together and rise above the tension, but it was easier said than done. I looked down at Dr. Harrison Daniels and all the bare skin showing. *Bear* skin. I awkwardly snorted and slapped my hand over my mouth. "Um, sorry. I seem to have a case of the giggles. This is where I get professional, though. I promise I'm usually a complete professional. And mature, too."

Dr. Daniels was so tall that the edge of the massage table hit him at midcalf. His broad shoulders tapered down to a trim waist and hips. The muscles in his back rippled when he moved, and his shoulders and arms flexed as I stepped around him. Every inch of his skin that I could see was deeply tanned, like he spent a lot of time in the sun. Naked. Freckles dotted his shoulders and upper back. A lone freckle was lower, in the center of one of the dimples of his lower back.

With a start, I realized I wanted to lick that lower freckle. All of them, really. I wanted to lick all of Dr. Daniels. My body buzzed with awareness, and I fought to get it under control.

"I've heard good things about you." Adjusting his position again, he let out a low growl and gripped my armrests more tightly.

I worried that I wasn't moving this along fast enough for him. He was a doctor. He was busy. He had maneuvered his schedule around to steal away for a well-deserved massage, obviously. I should stop wasting his time just staring at him.

"Are there any particular areas you'd like me to focus on?"

"Not particularly. Just do your thing." His voice was an even deeper growl.

Not wanting to keep him waiting any longer, I rubbed warmed oil into my hands and stood at the front of the table, my hips near his head. Leaning over, I placed my hands on his back and instantly felt a jolt of pleasure zing through me and shoot straight down my body to my toes. His warm skin and firm muscles were pliable under my hands, and I felt something that I could best describe as the buildup of an electric charge. Touching him felt a little like sticking my tongue to the tip of a battery. I'd done that when I was a kid at the urging of a neighborhood bully, but I'd found that I liked the sensation it gave me. I sure as hell liked the sensation I was getting from touching Dr. Daniels. The zingy-zapping was making my girly parts tingle.

He made a growly noise and that feeling heightened, but I fought it. I was a professional. I shook my head to clear the fog and clenched and unclenched my fingers before trying again. Palms flat on his back, I worked my fingers into his muscles. I leaned farther on him as I trailed lower, so tempted by that lone freckle. It wasn't until my pubic bone brushed against his thick hair that I realized how far into Lala-land I was.

Dr. Daniels let out a sound that could be described as a growl mixed with a groan, and his big hand whipped out to grip the back of my thigh. "Fern..."

I sucked in a deep breath and straightened. "I'm sorry. Sorry, I didn't mean for my...to make contact with your... Sorry. So sorry."

I stepped to the side of the table and carefully kept my body as far from his as I could while I worked his lower back. Lower, lower, the edge of the towel taunted me, begging me to slip my fingertips under it. I cleared my throat and forced my hands to stay in a neutral zone. I didn't know what the hell was wrong with me. Why was I acting like a complete perv?

I managed to keep myself together for a few more minutes, until I decided that massaging the backs of his thighs would be an awesome idea. It wasn't an area that I necessarily avoided on clients. The thighs held a lot of tension, but why I'd skipped straight there on this man, I had no clue. Yes, I did. Control. I had no self-control.

But, oh, he had thick, strong thighs, dusted with hair that tickled my wrists as I kneaded his hamstrings. It was insane. I was more turned on than I could ever remember being. My body was pulsing in time with the way I worked my hands over him. I was touching him again, leaning over him, my pelvis was practically riding his leg. I was crossing a line I'd never crossed.

"Jesus, woman." Dr. Daniel's rough voice startled me.

When he raised his upper body and captured my eyes with a heavy-lidded gaze, I snapped back to reality. Filled with horror, I backed away lifting my offending hands in the air. "I am so sorry. So very sorry. Please just get dressed. I'd understand if you filed a complaint. I'm not... I don't know what... I'll go. Oh god."

I had all but molested the man. I was so ashamed that I couldn't handle the idea of facing him a moment longer. I flew out of the room, slammed the door shut behind me, and came face to face with a room full of women who'd obviously been doing their best to over-hear what was happening in my back room. I let out a horrified little squeak.

"I need the rest of the day off. It's an emergency." With that, I raced out onto Main Street so mortified that I seriously considered picking up Kinsley and leaving the state.

If my gas tank wasn't nearly on E and my bank account balance wasn't $2.62, I probably would have. Instead, I ran down Main and rounded the corner onto Magnolia vowing that the first thing I was going to do when I reached my cottage was Google pediatricians in the area and find Kinsley a new doctor.

9

HARRISON

*T*wo days later, I was still trying to decide what approach to take with my mate. I'd stopped back at Jammie's Salon a few times between patients on both days trying to catch her, but she seemed to have some kind of radar tuned into me. Every time I showed up, she was either gone or busy with a client. I got a painful erection every time I thought about her, which was almost every moment of every day. I was ready to find her and make her mine. I'd waited long enough. I knew that she wanted me as much as I wanted her. The way the heat level of her massage amped up had proven that.

Fuck, I could still smell the delicious aroma of her arousal and I was dying to taste her on my tongue. Just the thought made me salivate. I was still beating myself up for not being quicker when I'd had the chance in the little massage room. Why hadn't I grabbed her, bent her over the little massage table, and proven to her that I was the man to make sure her needs were met? I would ease any ache, scratch any itch, and fulfill any desire she had. Always. I was ticked at myself that I botched my chance. When I had tried to reach for her in the massage room, she'd run out faster than a bolt of lightning streaking through the night sky.

I considered taking the day off and using it to stake out the salon, hang out until she had no choice but to see me. Unfortunately, there was a stomach virus going around the local elementary school and the clinic was swamped.

Fern. My beautiful human mate with the magic hands and a vintage name that fit her perfectly. To the Victorians, ferns had been a symbol of humility and sincerity.

"Are you seeing scheduled patients today, or are you planning to spend all day staring at the wall, lost in a daydream?" Polly stood in the doorway to my office with her hands on her hips.

I sighed. The problem was I couldn't focus. My mind wouldn't stop straying to Fern, and the longer I went without seeing her, the more I felt the need to find her. What if she was still stressing about the massage? I needed to reassure her, and she needed to know that we were mates. I had to make it clear that her massage was neither too provocative nor unwelcome—quite the opposite. Although, if that was how she massaged her other clients, we seriously needed to talk. That got me thinking about her placing her magic hands on other men and I let loose an angry growl before jumping up and rounding my desk.

"Hello? Earth to Dr. Grump?" Polly snapped her fingers. "Is your spaceship set to touch down on solid ground in *this* solar system any time soon?"

I grunted and sank into one of the chairs that faced my desk. "Why are these chairs here? I never have people in my office. What purpose do they serve? They're completely useless."

"Okay, I'm gonna get real with you here. You're acting like you're a few fries short of a Happy Meal. What gives?"

I let my head drop back and stared at the ceiling. "I met my mate."

"Yeah. And?"

Jerking upright, I wrinkled my brow. "You knew?"

"Of course, I knew. The whole island knows. After the two of you got all hot and bothered over at Jammie's, island gossip ran rampant. We're all placing bets on when y'all are gonna bump uglies. What are you waiting on?"

"*Bump uglies?*" I groaned at her crude expression. "And let's get one thing clear, we did not get hot and bothered. Who's been saying that?"

I hated the thought of rumors about Fern behaving unprofessionally in any way being spread through Sunkissed Key's gossip party line.

Rolling her eyes, Polly sighed and sat in my chair. "No one is saying anything derogatory about your girl. She's a doll. Had that daughter of hers mighty young, but things happen. Jammie speaks highly of her. Why haven't you tossed her over your shoulder and dragged her off to your den?"

"I don't have a *den*, Polly."

"You know what I mean."

"I've been swamped, you know that, and when I do get a minute and head over to Jammie's to talk to her, she's either locked in her massage room with a client or she's off the clock." I stood up and started pacing. "It's making me crazy."

"I noticed. We all have. Don't worry, though. I've been telling all your patients that you're fighting a migraine, so they'll forgive your jackassery."

"Are you serious?"

"Yep."

I closed my eyes and slapped a hand to my forehead, motioning her out of my office with the other. "Go. I'm done with this conversation. I'm getting back to work now."

"You better. I will not have this clinic fall apart on account of your raging pheromones." With that, she sauntered out of my office and didn't look back.

I resumed seeing my scheduled patients, starting with little Bradley George in exam room two, who threw up on his mom's shoes while I prescribed an electrolyte drink to keep him from dehydrating. In exam room three, I saw Tavion James, an older boy who had a little brother in elementary school. He stank like diarrhea and vomit, not unlike my other patients. After Tavion, I examined three more kids before I was caught up and able to disappear back into my office for a breather.

I settled into my desk chair with my head in my hands and closed my eyes. Immediately, memories of Fern's magic touches—like tonic for the soul—flooded my thoughts. When I heard her soft voice coming from the front desk, my first assumption was that I was hallucinating. I sat up straight and heard it again. A sweet, gentle sound with a hint of a southern drawl, it was definitely hers and definitely not a hallucination. I stood up so fast, my chair toppled over, and I hurried out of my office and down the hall to the reception desk.

There she was, my Fern, holding a basket of cinnamon rolls. She was trying to offer them to Polly as she nervously glanced back at the door like she couldn't wait to make a run for it. "I don't want to disturb him, really."

Polly laughed. "Too late."

Fern glanced over her shoulder. As I came toward her, her lips parted on a little gasp and the basket fell from her hands onto the edge of Polly's desk where it teetered for a moment before Polly caught it at the last second—just before the rolls went flying. "Um…"

I grabbed her upper arm and dragged her after me, down the hall and into my office. I had so much to say to her, but all of a sudden, my words left me and I couldn't think of a single one. I was too caught up in her deliciously sweet scent of wild honey and the silky feel of her skin as I held her arm.

"I don't… I think… I just came…" She kept starting and stopping sentences, but went silent when I pulled her through the doorway and kicked the door shut behind us.

Spinning her around, I pressed my body against hers pushing her against the closed door. Staring down at her, I watched as her pretty lips parted, before lowering my mouth to hers and gently nipping at her bottom lip. I sucked it, nibbled it, tasted it. She moaned as my tongue delved into her mouth and rolled over hers. My world had been off-kilter since I'd met her, but it was instantly righted by that first, delicious kiss.

Capturing her face between my hands, I devoured her like a desperate man. Two days had felt like two years, and my body yearned for hers as though she was the oxygen I needed to breathe.

She tasted like honey, and I stroked my tongue again over her sweet lips. I knew I'd never get enough of her. I would always want more. Fern wrapped her arms around my neck, pulling me closer and giving me the green light. While I explored her mouth, my hands ran over her hair and down her back. Her soft curves drove me wild. Her breathing hitched as I palmed her plump ass cheeks, giving them a little squeeze. Perfection. Her rounded backside was utter perfection. I lifted her so I could feel the heat between her thighs press up against my erection. I wanted to feel her, but I also wanted her to know what she did to me.

Fern's legs locked around my hips. Her hands locked in my hair, her fingers threading and tugging. Fierce kisses, her tongue stroking mine, her teeth nipping. She let out a husky little moan when she felt my erection press harder against her.

The world melted away. Nothing mattered but us—my mate and me. I didn't care where we were, who was in the building with us, I just needed to give and derive pleasure. Holding her tightly against me, I turned us to my desk and used my other arm to sweep it clear, scattering the contents on the floor. Still holding her with one arm, I sat her on the desk, and with my other arm, I reached over my head to drag my shirt up and off. I kissed and nibbled her throat while her hands stroked over my chest.

She mumbled something against my mouth. I slipped my hands under the hem of her shirt to her waist, electrified by her soft, warm, bare flesh beneath, when she said it again, louder.

"Wait."

10

FERN

*T*he last thing I wanted to do was to tell Harrison to stop. And he was now officially Harrison, versus Dr. Daniels, because the title "Dr." was reserved for those physicians who hadn't gotten to second base with me on top of their desks.

Harrison froze with his hands around my ribcage, just under my breasts. When I let go of his hair and lightly drew his wrists away, he dropped his hands and took a step back.

I had to say something. My mouth was too busy wanting to call him back or curse myself for stopping him. Without a doubt, I wanted him. He clearly wanted me as well. There was nothing wrong with two consenting adults going at it like animals in his office at the clinic during business hours. I mean, the door was closed. Yet…

"I didn't… I hadn't meant for this to happen." I cleared my throat and tugged the hem of my shirt down to cover my exposed midsection. "I only came to apologize. With cinnamon rolls. Homemade."

When he looked up at me skeptically, I cracked.

"Okay, *I* didn't make them. Susie did. I bought them from the Bayfront Diner. I don't know why I wanted you to think I made them." I tucked my hair behind my ear and wondered where my ponytail holder had disappeared to. "Well, that's a lie. I do know why. It's because you're so hot and so put-together and, for whatever reason, I act like such a hot mess around you."

"I like it." His voice was thick, husky, and his eyes were so black that I couldn't make out any of the brown in his irises. "I like everything about you."

"Bless you. That's sweet of you to say." I found my ponytail holder. It was on my wrist, so I quickly swept my hair into a bun. "I came to apologize for my unprofessional behavior during your massage. I really don't know what came over me, manhandling you that way. I've never done anything like that before. With anyone. I'll be 31 soon. Isn't that way too young for menopause? Yet I've been having hot flashes and I can't stop these feelings of extreme arousal. My hormones seem crazy. Could I be headed into early menopause? I don't know."

"It's not menopause."

"At any rate, I'm sorry. That's what I came to say. Although, I think we're even now since you kind of manhandled me back just now."

"Sorry." Judging by the tone of his voice, he wasn't sorry in the least. Not about manhandling me. The expression on his face said that the only thing he was sorry for was that he'd stopped.

"I liked it." I covered my face with my hands and groaned. "A lot. I didn't want to stop you."

He stepped closer again, he wasn't wearing a shirt and I was practically drooling at the firm musculature of his chest. The very large bulge in his jeans pressed against me. "I didn't want to stop, either. You did nothing to apologize for during that massage except run out of there. I wasn't attempting to make you stop, I was attempting to bring you closer. You know I'm a shifter, Fern. I have sharper-than-human senses. For instance, I can smell things that you can't. Like how aroused you are."

My eyes felt like they'd pop out of my head when his fingertips trailed up my inner thigh and close to my still very wet, very needy pussy. "What?"

"I can scent your—"

"No. Do *not* repeat that. Please. I'll die from embarrassment." I

47

waved my hands for him to stop, then flattened them on his chest, meaning to shove him away. His chest, though, was so solid, so strong, so hot. Instead, my fingers glided over his pectorals, feeling their contours. "I should go. You have patients."

"Polly cleared out the clinic as soon as I dragged you back here. We're alone, honey."

I swooned at the way his deep voice sounded when he said *honey*. "How do you know?"

He grinned, tapped his ear, and stole another kiss. "Still a shifter. I have lots of talents. I'm willing to give you a taste of a few of them right now."

I licked my lips and started to nod. "No! Wait. I didn't mean to nod. I can't. I can't have sex with you in your office. On your desk. I can't taste your talents. No matter how amazing that sounds."

Growling, Harrison held my hips, pulling me more snugly against him. "Okay."

I couldn't help but laugh when he didn't move away from me or step back. "This—this kind of thing is exactly how Kinsley happened."

More growls. "I don't want to hear about that. Not right now. Or ever. Whoever that asshole is better hope I never cross paths with him."

I wrinkled my nose but otherwise ignored his macho-man thing. I assumed he was merely attempting to make me feel special and unique by acting like he wanted to protect me or look out for me or something. "I just mean, this isn't me. I don't do this kind of thing—meet a man and then have sex with him. I don't do hookups. I made that mistake once, and I ended up pregnant with Kinsley. Not that *she's* a mistake. Unplanned, yes—mistake, no. I'm grateful for her. Most days. I am. Really. I just... After that, I haven't... I'm just not comfortable."

"It's not like that with me."

I found myself laughing again, fully enjoying how much he seemed to be into me. It was flattering. "I think I actually really like you. You were so good with Kinsley, even when she was being her difficult teenage self. You're attractive and kind. You have your life together, and everyone I know on this island seems to have made it a point to tell me what a stand-up guy you are. If you want to go out on a date with me, I'd do that."

He stopped and tilted his head to one side. "Did you just ask me out on a date?"

I blushed. "I know it's a little awkward, what with your boner pressing against my stomach and you smelling my...ugh...arousal... and all. But I don't sleep around. At all. No exceptions. I could date, though."

"I'd love a date with you."

I nodded, excited and a little shy all of a sudden. "Yeah? Cool."

He easily lifted me off of his desk and put me on my feet on the ground. "I'll pick you up tonight."

I found my body instantly aching to be pressed up against him again. "Oh shoot! Not tonight. I'm busy tonight. Kinsley bit me again last night and I grounded her. If I don't stay at the house to keep an eye on her, she'll leave."

He curled his lip. "She bit you?"

I waved it off. "It's fine. It was just a nip. She's grounded until next weekend. We could go out then."

"Maybe the three of us could hang out at your place tonight. Do you cook?"

I winced. "Not well."

"I'll cook, then. I'll come over and cook for you two, and I'll have a few words with your little wolf about keeping her teeth to herself." He looked over my hand and arms until he spotted the bruise on my fore-arm. "I could always bite her back for you."

I scowled at him, not realizing he was teasing until he winked and broke into a grin. Sighing, I swayed closer to him. "I'm taking care of it."

"Tell me your address."

"I'm still not sure this is a good idea. I can't seem to control myself around you." I found myself again pressed flush against him, of my own doing this time.

"Tell me where you live or I'll have to go into Polly's filing system to find out for myself. She won't be happy. Please do not inflict that woman's wrath upon me." He leaned down and kissed me softly, tenderly. "Tell me."

"Magnolia Street. We live on Magnolia Street. You can't miss us. We're the house with the harried and frazzled human mother and the sullen and angry wolf child."

He kissed me again, his hands sliding to grip my ass and squeeze it before he held me away. "Now, go. Get out of here. It's killing me to let you walk away from me right now. You should go while you still can."

Heaven help me, I believed him. With a smile as wide as the Atlantic on my face, I hurried out of his office, only stopping to glance back at him once. He was sexy as sin, standing in the middle of his office, his torso bare, his chest rising and falling with each quick breath. His eyes narrowed lustily. He growled and leaned forward as though poised to give chase. I squeaked, raced out the clinic door, and ran back to the salon, giggling euphorically the whole way.

HARRISON

*A*s soon as she saw me haul Fern off to my office, Polly had canceled all afternoon appointments and closed the clinic for the rest of the day. I went home and took an ice-cold shower then headed over to Fern's place. I was early for our date. Several hours early. She probably hadn't meant for me to come over right after work, but I was eager to see her again—for our *date.* I snorted a sharp laugh as I turned down Magnolia Street. A mate date. I'd never heard of mates dating before—they didn't need to. The outcome was inevitable. Forever bonded with the person who was your other half, the person who made you whole. But if Fern wanted a date, a date she would get—and as many as she fancied. I'd do whatever I had to win her over.

It was easy to tell which house was hers by the aroma of wild honey that surrounded it. The little cottage was smack dab in the middle of Magnolia. It faced the water, but the houses on the next street over, Shipwreck Way, blocked it from having a view that would raise its market value substantially. I parked my motorcycle in front of her house and groaned as the scent of sweet honey grew so strong, it entirely ruined the libido-dampening effects of the cold shower I'd taken.

A handful of neighborhood kids were hanging around playing kickball in the street and ran over as soon as they recognized me. I knew each of them by name, and their mothers, a few of whom followed their children and also headed toward me.

"Look at his Harley!" Darius Hendricks elbowed Jacob Conner before looking up at me with near hero worship in his eyes. "I want a ride, Dr. Daniels!"

I glanced at Fern's place and noticed the front door was opening. Instead of Fern emerging, Kinsley slipped out. Her eyes narrowed to slits when she saw me. Marching straight over to the little group that was forming around me, she dug her fists into her hips and glared at me.

"What are you doing here?"

"Can we ride it?"

"Yeah, can we?" Jacob ran his hand over the front fender and groaned. "Man, I can't wait until I'm old enough to own one of these bad boys."

"If you don't scram, you're never going to be old enough. Get the hell out of my yard." Kinsley turned her back to the kids and crossed her arms.

Darius's mom had reached the group just in time to hear Kinsley. Scowling, she put a hand on her son's shoulder. "Young lady, you best watch your tongue."

Kinsley was less than intimidated. "You can get out of my yard, too."

I cleared my throat. "Kinsley—"

Susan Bell approached with a disapproving glare at Kinsley. "Where is your mother? It's about time someone had a talk with her about your behavior. The whole neighborhood is tired of your attitude and your acting out." Susan glanced up at me and shook her head, like we were going to agree. "I don't know where these two came from, Dr. Daniels, but this neighborhood has gone downhill since they moved in."

"Come down off the high horse, you old hag. This neighborhood was a shithole before we moved in and it's still a shithole." Kinsley bared her teeth at Susan, and I watched Susan's fists ball up at her sides.

Stepping in, I took Kinsley's shoulders, spun her, and nudged her back toward her house. "Inside. Please. I know for a fact that you're already grounded. It's probably not the best idea to make it worse."

She started to growl, but, with my back to the group, I bared my own teeth at her. My threat was effective. She stomped off toward the house and slammed the door closed behind her.

"Good grief. That girl..." Susan fanned herself and turned to a few of the other neighborhood moms, exchanging sounds of outrage and disgust with them.

I folded my arms across my chest and turned a glare at them. "I've got a date to get on with. If you ladies will excuse me."

Susan's face turned red. "With *Fern*?"

As if on cue, the door behind me opened again and without turning to look, I sensed Fern moving toward me. A magnetic pull was compelling me to get closer to her. When she came to a stop beside me, she looked up at me with her big, emerald eyes. "What did she do this time?"

I wrapped my arm around her shoulders and pulled her closer. God, I'd missed her. It had only been a few hours, but the way my heart leaped with excitement at the sight of her made it seem like we hadn't seen each other for weeks. She was beautiful. Half of her hair was up in rollers, a faded bathrobe was tied at her waist, and one of her eyes was perfectly made up—only one. Her lips were bare and beckoned me to kiss the frown right off them.

"She called me an old hag after threatening Jacob and sassing Shanice." Susan's whiny voice interrupted the kiss I was about to plant on Fern and I wasn't too thrilled about it.

Fern's eyes widened as she gaped at Susan. "Oh, I'm so sorry. Truly, I apologize. She's under punishment and lashing out because of it."

Connie Conner, whose son Kinsley had threatened, piped up. "That girl is an absolute heathen. Whatever her *punishment* is, it ain't enough. You need to step it up a notch. She's gonna land her behind in juvie—"

I growled and pulled my mate into my side. "Last I checked, Connie, you hadn't earned yourself a degree in child psychology. If you don't mind, we're going to go inside and enjoy our date now."

I wasn't concerned in the least about burning bridges with Susan Bell, Connie Conner, or Shanice Hendricks. I was, however, concerned with the little crease worrying my mate's forehead. I led Fern up to her front door and gently ushered her through it, closing it behind me. "I just realized I forgot to stop at Mann Grocery for supplies. I was in such a hurry to get over here."

"What just happened?" Fern rubbed at the eye with makeup on it, smearing her mascara, and then gasped. "I'm not ready! You're early! Like..." She glanced at the clock on her microwave. "Three hours!"

I rubbed my thumb under her eye, wiping away the black smudged mascara and smiled down at her. I didn't know how I was supposed to keep my hands off her. "I was anxious to begin our date."

Her face warmed and her eyes blinked a few times before she sighed and pressed against my hand, which was still resting on her cheek. "I'm a mess. That seems to be my pattern whenever I'm around you."

"Mother!" A wild screech came from the back of the house. "Did you wash my blue shirt?! The one that Dee gave me? Oh my god, if you washed that shirt, I'm going to kill you!"

Fern's shoulder's stiffened and she sighed. "Maybe this was a bad idea. I don't know what made me think this would work out."

"And what is my doctor doing here?" Kinsley stormed out of her room and snarled when she saw me. "What are you doing here? Do doctors make house calls now or something?"

"Kinsley! Go back to your room."

"Oh my god. Are you hitting on him? My doctor? That's vile! What's wrong with you?!" The teen wore a look of pure disdain. "Can't I even have one thing that's just mine? One freaking thing? He was going to teach me wolf stuff, so you go and throw yourself at him. You can't stand not having all the attention focused on you, can you?"

I was half-shifted before I could control my bear. He let out a fierce growl and my dominance loomed over the room. "Do not talk to your mother like that."

Fern stared up at me with shocked eyes, her mouth hanging open. She took a step back and stumbled over a discarded pair of shoes.

I fought my bear back inside, using all of my willpower to gain control over him. When my claws retracted, I swallowed and rolled my neck. "Sorry."

Kinsley let out an angry wail and stomped back to her room, slamming the door hard enough to rattle the house. Sounds of things being thrown around came from behind the closed door, but Fern didn't seem fazed by it, as though that was normal.

She looked up at me. "That was... Wow."

I nodded. "I can't watch you be disrespected."

She snorted and rolled her eyes, breaking the tension. "You've come to the wrong house, then."

12

FERN

Suddenly exhausted, I stumbled over to the couch and sank onto it. I'd barely gotten a few deep, calming breaths in when I felt something seep through my robe, wetting my backside. I instantly knew what it was, because, well, that was just how my life rolled. Still, just to be sure, I stood up and bent over the couch cushion, daring a quick sniff. Pee. I sat in puppy pee. Terrific.

A dose of reality: I was dressed in nothing but a tattered old bathrobe, only half of my face had makeup and that half was smeared, and now I was wearing dog piss perfume. Also reality: my neighbors hated me, my daughter hated me, I wasn't sure how the puppy felt in that regard, and I. Was. Covered. In. Pee. In front of my date. A date who was way out of my league. A date whom I'd just witnessed half shift into the biggest grizzly bear I'd ever seen in the middle of my living room. Incidentally, that had been hot as hell.

Why did I think a date with a handsome, single doctor whose life was clearly orderly and systematic was a good idea? Me, queen of chaos and bedlam, ruler of pandemonium and disarray. Tears of frustration prickled my eyes and one leaked out, trickling down my cheek. I wiped it away with my sleeve and hurried into the kitchen to find something to scrub the couch with. That's when I discovered that the kitchen was a mess, too. Boots was in his open crate, eating a box of crackers—cardboard and all. The trash can was knocked over, and there was another puddle of pee on the floor.

I stopped and leaned against the wall. I'd had plans to clean the house…earlier. There were dishes piled in the sink, and it smelled like a dirty dog kennel. As embarrassed as I was to have Harrison see the state of my house, it was probably for the best. He needed to know the truth, and I wouldn't blame him one bit if he ran as fast and as far as he could.

I reached up to run my hand through my hair—and there were the rollers I'd forgotten about. With a heavy sigh, I buried my face in my hands. I was a hot mess. There was no hiding it for long. It was apparent in every aspect of my life. This was good, though. This was real. Once before, I'd fallen for a man way too fast—before I really even knew who he was. Ever since, I believed that it was better to be open and honest from the get-go rather than present a sugarcoated version of oneself.

"Hey, come here." Harrison had come up behind me and was pulling me into his arms, one big hand on the back of my rollers, gently pressing my face to his chest, the other stroking my back up and down, lower, and lower. It stopped moving entirely at the top of my ass. "What…"

"I sat in dog pee. The puppy's not quite housebroken yet and he peed on the couch. And tipped over the trash can. And he left a puddle in here, too. And there's a sink full of dirty dishes. And everyone in the neighborhood hates me."

At that moment, Boots seemed to decide that the stranger in the room was more interesting than the box of crackers he'd been intent on pulverizing, and he yelped excitedly. The little ball of fur came tumbling out, his tiny beagle body shaking with boundless enthusiasm. He jumped up on me, his sharp little puppy claws scratching my legs, then turned to Harrison, who, fortunately, was wearing jeans.

I smiled tightly, but I was ashamed. My house, my kid, even my puppy—it was all a mess. I just wasn't one of those people who could hold things together. I was imagining what it all must look like through Harrison's eyes, and it was not pretty. Not pretty at all.

"Okay, that's enough of that. Look at me." Harrison held my chin and lifted my face to his. "I want you to go take a hot shower—a leisurely one. Finish getting ready. Take your time. I'll take care of this."

I shook my head. "I can't let you do that. I'll clean this mess up."

"No. You have to care for yourself, first. You're stressed, over-whelmed, and you smell like pee. There's nothing wrong with letting someone offer a helping hand." Before I could protest again, he turned me around and gave me a push toward the back of the house. "Don't come back out here until you're calm and relaxed. I got this."

Bossy man. Pouting, I turned to look back at him. "I..."

"Go." He flashed a smile and winked. "I'll be here when you get back."

I paused again, just before I reached my bedroom door. "You don't have to stay, Harrison. No one would blame you, least of all me. This isn't paradise, and I know it's not what you were expecting."

His dark eyes flashed. "You don't know what I was expecting. You go take that shower, honey. I got this."

Feeling properly chastised, I ducked into my bedroom, slipped out of my robe, and tossed it into the hamper. In the bathroom, I let the water heat up before stepping under the steamy spray. By the time I washed off and slipped into the dress I'd picked out for our date, I was feeling lighter. I wasn't sure what I'd find when I went back out to the kitchen, but whatever it was, I'd pull up my big girl panties and deal with it. The house wasn't going to clean itself. Boots wasn't going to walk himself.

I left my face bare, and let my hair just dry naturally and do its thing. I was thrilled, if slightly surprised, when I stepped out of the bedroom to find that Harrison was still here.

He was sitting on the dry end of the couch petting Boots, who was in his arms. The soiled couch cushion was missing and the room had been tidied. Boots, normally a rambunctious, wiggly ball of energy, was calmly giving Harrison kisses on the chin. A candle was lit on the coffee table, and as I moved toward the duo, I did a double-take at the kitchen. Clean. Completely. Dishes done and put away, trash picked up, floor washed, and another lit candle on the counter.

My heart wedged in my throat. This was completely unexpected. No man had ever done anything like this for me before. As I swallowed back the lump that tried to choke me, Harrison rose and came toward me. Boots trotted right alongside him and stopped when Harrison stopped.

"I wanted to wait until you finished to let you know that I'm heading to the grocery store to grab some stuff to make for dinner."

My mouth opened and I had every intention of thanking him verbally, but the next thing I knew, I had fisted the front of his shirt, and I was pulling his face down to mine to plant a passionately grateful kiss on the amazing man's mouth. Harrison moaned against my mouth, sending tingles coursing through me. His arm wrapped around me as I pushed him against the side of the fridge, threading my fingers in his hair so I could deepen our kiss.

His hands slid down, locking on my ass, and he lifted me so I was pressed against him intimately. I felt a wildness in myself that I'd never experienced, a need that overwhelmed common sense. The attraction had gotten even stronger than it had been in his office.

He moved us so I was sitting on the counter with his body wedged between my legs. We were making out like teenagers, and I had a compelling urge to taste him, to bite and nibble and give him a hickey like we were in high school.

"Are you kidding me?! Are you two going to have sex in the kitchen? I can hear every single thing you're doing!" Kinsley's angry voice shattered the mood and snapped me back to reality.

I quickly pushed Harrison away and hopped off the countertop, smoothing my dress and trying not to die of embarrassment. I felt like I'd just been caught by the prison warden as I attempted a jailbreak.

"I vaguely regret teaching her how to fine-tune her sense of hearing." Harrison pulled me back against his chest and bent his head so his lips were next to my ear. "Later."

I pushed him away again and ran my hands through my hair. "Don't bet on it."

Grinning, he lifted an eyebrow. "Challenge accepted."

"I can still hear you and it's still disgusting!" Kinsley appeared in the kitchen doorway and scowled at me. "You wait until I'm fifteen to turn into a slut? I'm not having a little sibling now!"

I snapped into serious-mom mode, temporarily forgetting the delicious man making panty-melting propositions to me. "First of all, young lady, you watch your mouth. Second, call me a slut again and you'll be grounded for a month. Third, go to your room and stay there."

"Great. Banish me to my room so you can screw my doctor on the kitchen table. Is that the plan? I can't believe you!"

Harrison growled, but I held up my hand. I was her mother and her attitude was mine to handle. "Two weeks, now. No screens, no hanging out after school with your friends."

"I hate you!" Kinsley screeched and stormed off to her room, slamming the door shut and rattling the entire house.

I sighed and turned back to Harrison, all the tension from earlier was back in full force. "I'd love to be able to say that this isn't the norm, but the truth is, it's pretty much always a barrel of laughs around here."

He frowned, his eyes on the spot where Kinsley had just been. "It's not easy to watch her behave that way."

"It's not all that easy for me, either—and I *love* her. I don't know what else to do with her. I'm really hoping she'll grow out of this anger and defiance. And out of hating me. In the meantime, though, this is my reality and she's my responsibility. If by chance you decide you're going to hang around for a while, you can't go threatening her with your big, growly bear. I can't have you coming in and disciplining her, even if she deserves it. That has to be my job because when you decide you're done with me, I'll still be here parenting her."

He shook his head. "That's just it, Fern. I'm never going to be done. Not with you, or with Kinsley."

13

HARRISON

I sat in my office leaning back in my desk chair and trying to focus on the bills in front of me. Despite them being normal monthly expenses and despite having done the same thing every Saturday afternoon for years, I couldn't focus past the first one. I couldn't stop thinking about Fern. She was a conundrum—delicate, soft spoken, but strong as steel at the same time. She'd gone through almost every emotion last night, but she'd still managed to put on a pleasant face as she ate dinner across from me. Even though Kinsley had not let up all through dinner.

She was frazzled, that much was evident. Kinsley had done a good job of wearing her mother's nerves thin, but it needed to stop. I understood what Fern had said about disciplining being her job, and I respected it. On the other hand, I was her mate and I was going to be in her and Kinsley's lives, whether Kinsley liked it or not. I wasn't going to step on Fern's toes, and I wasn't going to pretend to be Kinsley's father, but the girl had to learn to treat her mother with respect. It drove my bear crazy to see how Kinsley treated our mate. Yet, he was fond of the child. We both were. After all, we had a connection to her as well. We needed to come up with a clever way to help.

First, I had to come up with a way to tell Fern that we were mates.

I was almost hesitant to, though. She was stressed and exhausted from dealing with her daughter, and I wasn't sure she even knew what mates were. How would she handle the news that I was going to be a permanent fixture in her life? It was a big change. I wanted to think she'd embrace it as a positive change. I knew it would be for me, but Fern had been alone with her daughter for a long time. Just how long, I wasn't certain, but it was evidently a conscious choice. She was beautiful, hardworking, loving, and kind. If she hadn't chosen to be single, she wouldn't be. If she so much as snapped her fingers, men would line up for a chance to take her out.

I growled at the thought. All the emotions and instincts that come with finding a mate had kicked in full force for me. I was possessive and jealous. I didn't like the idea of anyone else looking at her, much less touching her. I couldn't wait for her to wear my scent—and my claiming mark. The fact that I'd made it to the office instead of following the strong urge I'd had to go straight over to her house that morning was a miracle. I needed to see her again. I'd had to leave her house the night before with just a chaste kiss on the cheek because Kinsley had planted herself on the couch, arms crossed, mean-mugging Fern and had refused to move. Fern wasn't keen on the two of us displaying affection in front of her teenage daughter, and I couldn't blame her for that. But I ached to have more of her.

I rolled the kinks out of my neck and shoved the paperwork aside. My bear wanted to run, but I wasn't that stupid. If I let him take control, he'd beeline it straight to Fern's front door. I stood up to stretch my legs when I heard a knock at the front door. The clinic closed at noon on Saturdays, but a deep inhale told me that it was Kinsley.

A rush of panic shot through me. Was something wrong with Fern? I hurried to the front and threw open the door. I looked behind Kinsley, down the street left and right, then ran my eyes over her to check for any injuries. "What's the matter?"

She rolled her eyes and squeezed past me. "Nothing. God. You're wound as tight as my mom."

"Is she okay?"

"Um. I guess. Although, she's probably gonna throw a shit-fit when she wakes up and finds me gone." She grunted. "Can you believe she grounded me for another week?"

Realizing that nothing catastrophic had occurred, I relaxed a bit. "You're lucky she didn't let me hang you upside down by the ankles and shake you until your brain wiggled into place and you learned to play nice. I offered."

"What. Ever." She walked behind Polly's desk and plopped down into her chair.

"To what do I owe this unexpected visit?"

Spinning back and forth, she looked like she was chewing on a mouth full of words that didn't taste very good. "What are your intentions with my mom?"

Taken aback, I didn't answer.

"She's annoying as hell and I can't stand her most of the time, but if you're just trying to get a piece of ass and then move on, you should know that I know people who could beat the shit out of you."

I barked a laugh, unable to help it. "Wow."

"It's not funny. I'm serious." She scowled at me. "If you hurt her, I will hurt you."

"I see. So she's not so bad, huh? If you're not careful, someone might suspect that you might even care about her a little. I mean, if you're here, willing to fight a grizzly for her and all." I grinned at the girl, a warmth blooming in my chest. "Well, you don't have anything to worry about, Kinsley. When it comes to your mom, the last thing in the world I want is for her to be hurt, by me or anyone else. She's my mate."

She frowned. "Your mate? What the hell is that supposed to mean?"

It was my turn to frown. I pulled one of the waiting-room chairs over and sat down, facing her. "Apparently, there's a lot about shifters that you don't know yet."

"So? What's it mean? Your *mate?*"

I leaned back and ran my hand through my hair, thinking of how to explain a shifter mate bond to a fifteen-year-old who'd never seen it happen before. "One of the special things about being a shifter is that you have one other person in the world that is fated to be your partner, your life companion, your *mate*. My parents are mates. They've been together for fifty years and still have that over-the-moon, butterflies-in-the-tummy kind of love like they had when they were kids. It's like love at first sight, but better. A mate, when you have one, will be so special to you that they will take precedence above anything or anyone else."

"My mom is yours?" She seemed skeptical.

"Yes, she is. She doesn't know it yet, though. Humans don't have the ability to instinctually sense it like we shifters do. I knew the moment I laid eyes on your mom that she was my one and only. She was made for me." I saw that Kinsley wanted to argue, but I pressed on. "I was made for her, too. Your mom is the only woman in this world I want by my side—the only woman I will ever want. I was just thinking about how to explain all that to her when you knocked."

She leaned forward and rested her elbows on Polly's desk. "So, you like…want to marry her?"

I shrugged. "If she'll have me. Marriage is a human institution, though. Shifter mates usually mark each other. It's how they claim one another and bond themselves together forever. Whether she accepts me or not, there will never be anyone else for me. Until the day I die, your mom will be the only woman for me."

"What about that old hag, Susan Bell, who was drooling over you yesterday? Or the other moms who talk about how hot you are behind your back? You're not going to nab yourself a side chick when you get bored with my mom, are you?"

I leaned forward, too. "That's not even a possibility."

"So, what, you're like going to try to be my dad, now?"

I grunted. "I'm not going to try to be anything but what I am, and I'm not your dad. I get the feeling that you don't want me to be, either."

Kinsley's eyes narrowed, and she sat back and spun around. "I don't need a dad. I had one. He was an ass. He knocked Mom up and then left before I was born, even though he knew about me. Mom doesn't talk about him, but I found his name from one of Mom's old yearbooks a few years ago. I called him, and he said he always knew I'd call one day, but he had no interest in being anyone's dad and he wasn't going to send money to pay for me just because my mom was dumb enough to get herself knocked up."

I saw red for a moment. "What's the fucker's name?"

Kinsley spun back around, grinning. "I think I like you. Are you going to treat my mom good?"

"Better than good. And I really do want that fucker's name."

"Maybe I'll give it to you if you teach me more about being a shifter. Not at some lame appointment, though. I don't want my friends to see me coming out of the Children's Clinic—I'm fifteen for god's sake."

I found myself tempted to take a page from her book and roll my eyes at her. "Deal. But only if your mom says it's okay."

"Ugh. Fine."

"And before I agree to shifter lessons, you're going to have to agree to adjust the rude 'tude and be a whole lot nicer. You keep disrespecting your mom and I will shift into my bear and eat you like a snack. Do you understand me?"

She just rolled her eyes and stood up. "What. Ever. Like you even could."

I grinned. "Lesson number one: Don't start a fight you can't win."

FERN

I woke up late on Saturday after spending most of the night tossing and turning, dreaming of Harrison, and waking up periodically completely aroused and covered in a sheen of perspiration. I was restless and achy with need, a feeling I'd never experienced before. It was baffling. I'd never reacted to a man like I was reacting to him.

I had to take a cold shower and dress in a loose sundress because I was in such a heightened state of sensitivity that even the fabric on my skin was irritating. I also craved whipped cream. And chocolate. Instead of finding the kitchen a mess and Boots whining to get out, I found the dishes done, the crate empty, and a note on the counter.

Kinsley had taken him out front to walk him and play a little. She did her dishes, was exercising the pup, *and* left me a note to explain her absence? Had I entered the Twilight Zone? I fought the chocolate craving, slipped my feet into a pair of flip-flops and went out to find her.

She wasn't in the front. I found her in the back, playing fetch with Boots, tossing his ball back and forth, even retrieving it herself when Boots wouldn't cooperate and instead just rolled over and begged for belly rubs. When she noticed me on the back porch, she actually smiled. Oh, I was definitely in an alternate dimension.

My heart leaped into my throat and my jaw dropped. For a moment, I got a glimpse of my sweet little girl, the Kinsley before she became the hormonally charged adolescent monster.

Kinsley scooped up Boots and brought him up to the porch. "Hey."

I swallowed the lump that had formed in my throat. "Hi there. Thanks for taking care of Boots this morning."

"Well, he is my dog." Her sharp tone was back, but she immediately cleared her throat and started again, lighter. "It's what I'm supposed to do."

I wrapped my arms around my waist and smiled at my baby girl, praying that this was a sign her anger was finally fading. "Can I make you some lunch?"

"Do I look like I want food poisoning? Hard pass." She rolled her eyes and shoved Boots at me. "I'm going to listen to music in my room."

I just nodded and took the pup, angling sideways so she could step around me. Well, it wasn't a complete 180, but Kinsley did seem like she was trying to be more pleasant. It was obviously hard for her, but the effort was there.

"Oh yeah, would it be cool if Doc Daniels came over and gave me shifter lessons?" She tossed the question out as though it was an offhand thought, but I could sense her tension riding on it.

I let Boots lick my cheek and stared out at the yard. "Instead of at his clinic?"

"Yeah. Not a big deal at all, right?"

There was a sudden knot in my stomach. "Let me think about it, okay?"

"Fine. What. Ever." The door slammed—an audible end to Kinsley's pleasant behavior.

I blew out a long breath and looked up at the clear, blue Florida sky. I had no reason to feel panicked, did I? I'd been fine with allowing Kinsley to go to Harrison's office and learn about being a shifter.

Having lessons at our house, though, that somehow seemed so much more…personal.

I'd been careful not to get close to any man over the past fifteen years. We were a family, Kinsley and I, and I wanted her to grow up with that kind of stability. I didn't want her world upended by having her get attached to someone who was just going to leave in the end. She didn't deserve that kind of heartbreak. It terrified me to think of her getting too close to Harrison. His walking away might devastate her. As her mom, it was my duty to protect her from that.

Fern, I'm never going to be done.

The memory of Harrison's words rolled over me like an ocean wave. He'd sounded so sure when he'd said it. I huffed a laugh. We'd only had one shitty date, and he had the nerve to declare he wasn't going anywhere. As though he could predict what the future held.

No matter how good it felt to hear that he wanted to stick around, I wasn't about to pin my hopes and dreams on it. I hugged Boots, petting him with my cheek. I wasn't ready to give Harrison up yet, either. I really wanted to give whatever this attraction was between Harrison and me a chance to play itself out. What I wouldn't do, however, was fool myself into believing that he would never leave. I'd done that once before. I wasn't stupid enough to make that mistake twice.

Listening to Kinsley slamming and banging things around inside the house, I released another sigh. If Harrison promised to continue giving Kinsley lessons regardless of the direction our relationship took, even if we crashed and burned, I'd agree. I'd let her have the lessons at our house. She really needed some guidance from another shifter and I, as her mother, was responsible for seeing that she got it.

I'd just stepped foot into the house when Kinsley's arm shot out, nearly smacking me in the face with my phone. I took it from her, frowning, as she stormed off and slammed her bedroom door. I set Boots on the floor while checking the display. It was a call from Laila. "Hey! Is everything okay?"

Laila growled. "I think your child just called me a nasty name."

I sank onto the couch and groaned. "I'm sorry, Laila. I'll talk to her."

"No worries. I'll talk to her. I planned to have a little she-wolf to she-wolf chat with her anyway. There are a few tidbits of wisdom about being a female wolf shifter I'd like to pass along." She sighed. "Not why I'm calling, though. The real reason I'm calling is to tell you that you're invited to girl's night tonight and you can't say no. You need to cut loose with friends and have a little fun. Parker agrees. In fact, we *all* need a night out."

"I wish I could. My sweet and pleasant child is grounded, though. I can't leave the house, or she'll leave the house, too."

"Already thought of that. Maxim is working tonight, so Parker had to find a babysitter for Stella. Bring Kinsley over to Parker's house."

"Ha! Are you prepared for World War III? No way I can send Kinsley to Parker's with a sitter. She'd probably slip the sitter a roofie, steal their car, and go for a joyride around the island."

Laila snorted. "I'd like to see her try."

"I wish I could go. I think I could use some socializing and a drink or two."

"Bring her over. She'll like the babysitter, trust me."

I stared at Kinsley's bedroom door as the wheels in my brain turned. I could offer to take a week off her grounding if she behaves. Ugh! God, what kind of parent was I that I was thinking of letting my kid get away with calling me a slut just so I could have a night on the town? I could use the lessons with Harrison as leverage. I wouldn't even feel guilty for doing it. If she's not mature enough to behave herself for a few hours so I could have a much-needed evening to myself, then she's not mature enough to warrant the privilege of the lessons she wants. Right? "Fine. I'll do it."

"Yay! Parker lives on Shipwreck Way, only a street over from you and a couple of blocks down. It'll be the house with the perturbed-looking wolf in front of it."

"Wait, why are you going to be perturbed?"

She giggled. "It's not me. It's Gray. He's the babysitter."

I coughed a laugh imagining her very handsome, very mysterious boyfriend babysitting. "Are you sure he won't leave you after you pawn my daughter off on him?"

"I'm sure. We're stuck like glue. Meet us at nine."

I gasped. "Nine? What are we, teenagers? I'm normally in bed by ten."

"Not tonight, you're not. Tonight you're going to live a little, Fern. Get ready to par-tay!"

After hanging up, I hesitated just a moment before calling Harrison. He picked up on the first ring and the sound of his deep voice sent butterflies aflutter in my stomach. "Hi."

"Couldn't stay away from me, could you?"

Grinning like an idiot, I caught myself twirling a strand of hair around my finger. "I have a question for you."

"Proposing already? In that case, the answer is yes."

"Stop." Cheeks burning, I giggled like a schoolgirl. "I just wanted to know how you'd feel about working with Kinsley on her wolf shifter stuff over here. At my house, I mean."

He let out a soft snort of a laugh that sent tingles through me. "Sure."

"There's a follow-up question." I sucked in a deep breath. "Will you keep working with her even if this dating thing doesn't work out between us? I don't want to agree to it unless I know that you won't disappear on her because of me."

"I'm never going anywhere, honey."

I let out a breath that was too audible. "Okay, good! Great! Um, gotta go!"

I hung up the phone and slumped back on the couch grinning as I replayed his final words in my head. They were warm and comforting like being wrapped in a warm down comforter on a chilly night. *I'm never going anywhere, honey.*

FERN

*L*aila and Parker had reserved a big table at the back of Mimi's Cabana for us. I'd never been inside the place before, but I instantly took a liking to the owner, Mimi, and to its atmosphere, which screamed Polynesian tiki bar. I was surprised to find that they'd planned a bigger get-together than I thought. I was introduced to Hannah, Grace, Heidi, Kerrigan, and a very pregnant Megan. They were obviously all close friends and at first I felt slightly like an outsider. A little shy, I sat back and observed their interaction.

Parker noticed I was quiet and leaned into me. "What's happening with the good doctor?"

Even though she whispered, everyone's attention suddenly snapped to me. Laila grinned as Hannah leaned in quizzically. "The good doctor?"

"Doctor Harrison Daniels, Stella's new pediatrician. A big, handsome bear shifter—grizzly, not polar." Parker sighed. "I was trying to get him to sign up for Cybermates, but he found his mate before I had the chance to, apparently."

I felt my face burn. "No, it's…"

"It's what?" Laila laughed. "I still want the deets about happened in that massage room."

"In what massage room?" Grace waved her hands in the air and shook her head. "What did I miss? Tell me all the juicy gossip and don't leave any of the smutty parts out."

"Fern here had Dr. Daniels on her massage table until something or another went down and she ran out of there like her butt was shooting flames."

Heidi giggled. "Was it? Sometimes these bears can get carried away with their love spanks."

My head felt like it might explode. I took another shot of the strong tequila they all seemed to like and coughed. "*Love spanks?*"

Parker waved it off. "I'm sure if you and Harrison decide to experiment with spanking, you'll love it."

Laila was really having a good laugh by then. "You should see your face!"

"Let's get back to Dr. Harrison Daniels. Are you two a thing? I've met him." Hannah wagged her eyebrows. "He's so handsome. I know a few moms on this island whose kids only need one or two more illness before they're diagnosed with Munchausen by proxy because of that man. Mom's love him, if you know what I mean."

I shrugged and had to hold back a monstrous wave of jealousy. "We're dating, I guess."

"Dating?" Parker scowled.

"Things got kind of heated between us right away, but I put a halt to it. I told him I wanted to date first. He came over last night and cooked dinner for me." I made a face. "Well, for me and Kinsley. She made the evening a little tense. And she called me a slut."

Laila growled. "That girl! *She* could use a spanking. And not the fun kind."

Parker grunted. "Kids can sure be cockblockers."

"Are you and Maxim not getting enough sexy time?" Kerrigan sounded like she didn't think that was a possibility.

"We're barely having sex once a day anymore. I'm so tired and Stella has some sort of sixth sense that kicks in whenever Maxim comes near me. One good ass-grab and she instantly starts screaming."

"Once a day?!" I couldn't help but raise my voice. The tequila was already getting to me. "Once a day, *every* day?"

"Yeah... How often do you have sex?"

"Once..." I snorted. "Ever."

Hannah screamed. Actually screamed. "No!"

Laila shook her head. "No. Not possible."

Parker just gaped.

"I got pregnant with Kinsley my first time. That kind of soured me to the whole idea of sex from then on. Plus, I was pregnant, then there was childbirth, postpartum, single parenthood... I don't know. The whole idea of dating got pushed to the back burner. Very, very far back. Like a burner in another state." I shrugged and drank another gulp of tequila. "I seriously never even wanted to have sex again. At all. Until recently." Another swallow of tequila. "I want to sleep with Harrison, though, and I think I'm going to."

The table erupted in whoops and cheers. Heidi held up her drink. "To our new bestie, Fern, getting laid by the good doctor!"

They all clanked glasses in a toast to that sentiment and spent a good several minutes teasing me about it before the topic of conversation broke off into other things. I seemed to be the lightweight of the group—good and tipsy before anyone else. My lips were numb. I excused myself and hid in the ladies' room. Leaning up against the sink, I pondered my life and the direction it was taking.

It'd been so long since I'd gotten drunk, and at that moment, it felt nice. It also lowered my inhibitions and made me crave Harrison something fierce. Despite knowing better, I pulled my phone from my purse and dialed him. As soon as he answered, I giggled.

"Fern?"

"Harrison."

"Are you okay?"

"Mm-hm. I'm drunk."

"Where are you? Are you at home?"

I giggled again. "Nope. I went to the bar with my new girlfriends. I'm in the bathroom."

"You good?"

I sighed. "I'm good. But I'd be better if you were here."

"Don't do that to me, honey." He groaned. "You're killing me."

I bit my lip. "Want to come and get me?"

"What bar?"

"Mimi's Cabana. Are you coming?"

"I'll be right there."

I grinned. "You're so hot. I mean *nice*. I meant to say you're so *nice*."

Chuckling, Harrison hung up and left me leaning against the sink, wondering what I was going to do when he got here and whether I'd regret my actions in the morning when I was sober.

When I returned to the table, Laila eyed me with a curious expression on her face. "What'd you just do? You look guilty as hell."

"I might've called Harrison. He's on his way."

Parker laughed. "You drunk-dialed in secret! Party foul. We weren't there to stop you."

"Well, I said I was going to the ladies' room. Y'all could've followed."

They all laughed and Hannah stood up and grabbed my hand. "It's totally our fault, but instead of focusing on our shortcomings, new friend, let's dance until your man arrives to ravage you."

I swayed to the music but shook my head. "Oh no, I don't think there will be ravaging."

"Girl, you booty-called him! There will be ravaging."

"Maybe just a little third base." I thought about it and flushed. "Yeah, third base would be okay."

"What the fuck is a little third base?" Grace danced next to me, her eyes dancing with humor.

"I don't know, like a little bit of...like...just a little bit..."

Laila held my hips and swayed with me. "There's no such thing as a little bit of third base. I mean, can you suck a penis a little bit?"

Parker danced on my other side. "Or eat a—"

"Hello, ladies." Harrison's deep voice cut her off and sent a delicious tingle down my body and straight to my girly parts.

I turned and all but leaped into his arms. Wrapping myself around him, I looked up at him and smiled. "Do you think there's such a thing as a little bit of third base?"

He arched a brow. "I think it depends on why you're asking."

"Come with me, I'll tell you." I took his hand and pulled him after me into the dimly lit back hall. I grinned up at him. "Just a little bit?"

16

HARRISON

groaned and braced my hands on either side of her head. As drunk as she seemed to be, Fern's slender fingers were surprisingly swift and deft as they caught my belt buckle and tugged it open. My mouth went dry and I almost died right there—I wanted to kill myself after the words fell from my mouth next. "Fern, honey, stop."

She looked up at me with the sexiest pout. "Why? Don't you want a little bit of third base? Am I rushing you? We can stop at first and second along the way."

I swore and wrapped my arms around her waist. "I'm not doing a little of anything with you while you're drunk."

"I'm not that drunk." She tried making a stern face and giggled. "Okay, I'm drunk. But that doesn't mean I don't want to do this."

"How about you sleep on it, and if you still want to do this, you call me in the morning and I'll rush right over?"

She slumped into me. "I can't talk you into it?"

Laughing, I pressed a kiss to the top of her head. "Not while you're in this condition. At least, not for our first time."

"Fine. Will you take me home, then?" She made a show of redoing my belt, but every other movement had her hands bumping against my rock-hard erection. It was painful, to say the least.

"Of course."

"Thank you for coming to get me."

"Any time, any day."

I led her out of the back hall and toward the exit. Halfway there, the group of women who Fern had been with cornered me. Parker was there, leading the group. Another woman, one who worked at Jammie's Salon with Fern, somehow managed to snatch Fern and pull her aside, leading her a few feet away from me.

I kept one eye on Fern as Parker looked up at me with her hands on her hips. "What are your intentions with Fern, mister? I mean, *doctor*."

I almost laughed. That was the second time I'd been asked that question. I was glad, too. It showed how much people cared about my mate. "My intentions are to take her home safely and tuck her into bed. Alone."

"Not what I meant and you know it."

"If you're not serious about her, you need to step down. We'll take her home."

A tall, very pregnant woman wagged her finger at me. "Are you serious about her?"

"As a heart attack. She's my mate."

The tall woman inhaled sharply, and a smile stretched across her face. Parker cheered. "Yay! That's great. We thought so, but we wanted your confirmation. Well, get on out of here with her. What are you waiting for? Can't you see that your mate is tired and ready to leave?"

I watched as Laila hugged Fern and then shoved her over toward me. "She's had a bit too much to drink tonight, and it seems my friend here is a lightweight."

I nodded. "I got her."

"You'd better. We have an entire small army of polar bears and wolves at our disposal."

I pulled a card from Kinsley's deck and rolled my eyes. "And you can tell them to stand down. No one will protect Fern as fiercely or as loyally as I will. That, I promise you."

She nodded. "That's what we wanted to hear."

Fern's eyes darted between us and she raised her eyebrows. "I'm right here. I can hear all of you. I may be drunk but I'm not a child. I can take care of myself."

As she swung her arms emphatically, she stumbled over her own feet, but I caught her just before she went down. Grinning, I scooped her up and carried her out of the bar into the cool night air, which was much more pleasant than the stuffy bar.

Fern let out a happy sigh. "We're totally going to sleep together."

I grinned so wide that my cheeks hurt. "Yes, we are."

"It's going to be epic, isn't it?" She stroked my jaw and her head fell against my shoulder. "You have a great ass. Do you know that?"

I opened my truck, placing her on the passenger seat. When I reached for the buckle, she pushed my hand away and scooted to the center of the bench seat. I buckled her in there instead and walked around to the driver's side, grinning like a lovesick fool. As I got in, Fern instantly molded herself to my side.

"I meant what I said about your ass. It's great."

Laughing, I wrapped my arm around her shoulders and held her as I drove toward her house. "Thank you. So is yours."

"Did you know that some couples have sex once a day or more? Like every day?" She hiccupped. "That's a lot of practice. I've only tried it once, but I think I could be okay at it. With practice. Especially if I was practicing with you. You are a giant turn-on."

The truck swerved a little as I jerked. Tightening my grip on the wheel, I cleared my throat and shifted to ease the pressure in my pants. "You're going to be amazing."

"Shouldn't we just, like, practice?" She rested her delicate hand on my thigh. "Just a little?"

"Not until you sober up."

"Oh, come on." She grunted. "Please?"

Melting under her soft plea, I just held her more tightly and turned on Magnolia. As I figured she would, she fell asleep before I even pulled up in front of her house and shifted into park. When I asked her where Kinsley was, she stirred a little and mumbled something unintelligible.

I carried her into the unlocked house, something we'd be discussing later, and to her bedroom. I didn't allow myself to look around her personal space any more than was necessary. I wanted to see and know and learn everything about her, but only when she was ready. I slipped her sandals off, tucked a pillow behind her to keep her lying on her side, and pulled the blankets up to her chin before placing a wastebasket beside her in case she felt sick. I stood and watched her for a minute, grinning at how adorable she was, before leaving to find Kinsley.

She was easy enough to find by scent—just a street over and a couple of blocks down in a nice house right on the water. There was a mingling of scents around the home. Besides Kinsley's, Parker's was strong, as was her infant's, Stella. There was also a scent of bear—polar bear—which I assumed was Parker's mate since he was a member of a group of polar bears who had recently relocated to Sunkissed Key. When I knocked, the door was opened by a wolf shifter who wore the scent of Fern's work friend. The guy had a dark scowl on his face and glitter sprinkled everywhere else.

"I'm picking up Kinsley."

"Thank god! Normally, I would ask your name and check your ID, but nope. Take her. If you're kidnapping her, heaven help you."

"I can hear you!" Kinsley marched out of the house in a gust of indignation and glitter. "Hey, Doc. Can you believe this goof worked for the CIA?"

I stifled a laugh. "Come on, trouble. Time to get you home."

"Where's my mom?"

"In bed already." I nodded a thanks to the poor guy, who looked like he'd just descended to the bowels of hell and back, and Kinsley and I walked back to her house. "So, you tortured an ex-CIA agent? Why doesn't that surprise me?"

"They thought I needed a babysitter. Do you know how insulting that is?" She scoffed. "He'll be cleaning glitter out of his hair for months."

I winced. "That's rough."

"He treated me like I was a child."

"Ah. So, it was a justified glitter assault?"

"Without a doubt."

I followed her up the stairs and into her house. "Does Boots need to go out?"

"Yeah. I'll take care of it."

"I'll stay until you're finished. Then, you're going to lock this door. Do the two of you usually leave it unlocked?" I grunted and palmed my forehead. "I'm turning into my father."

"Gross."

I grunted again and waited as she took the puppy out back to do his business while I did my best to ignore my bear's demands to crawl into bed next to my mate and hold her while she slept. As much as I wanted to, I would wait.

17

FERN

I was never drinking tequila again. After throwing up all morning, my stomach finally settled enough for me to pop a couple of ibuprofen. I suffered a hangover all day on Sunday, which resulted in me making a solemn vow never to set foot in Mimi's again. Unless it was for a very good reason and there was no tequila.

By the time I got to work on Monday morning, I felt better for the most part. My morning was fully booked, but after lunch, I only had a few clients scheduled. I had time to sit with Laila and chat about Saturday night. They'd stayed out much later than I had and had a wild time that only ended when their men came and got them.

Laila also informed me that Gray no longer wanted children, thanks to Kinsley. She'd not only managed to cover the man in glitter but also proceeded to mock him mercilessly about how a pro spook had allowed a "child" to sneak up and glitter bomb him. Gray had not been at all amused. Laila and I, however, got a good laugh. When her attacks weren't focused on me, I could almost appreciate my child's moxie.

When the conversation turned to me, I was evasive. Some of the night was a blur. I vaguely remembered propositioning Harrison, and that he'd turned me down. In fact, I'd spent a good deal of Sunday stressing over that. What happened after, though, was a blank. I'd surmised that he'd taken me home and tucked me into bed before getting Kinsley. It made me break into a sweat just thinking about being in my bedroom with Harrison. The fact that I'd been too drunk to even remember it was a shame.

After Laila finished with her last client, she dragged me into her chair. While she worked on my hair, she pelted me with questions about Harrison.

"What did he say? How did he tell you—the exact words? I mean, he told the entire bar, so I'm assuming he told you. What are your plans?"

"What are you talking about?"

"Don't play coy with me, sister. He confirmed to everyone at Mimi's that you're his mate."

I frowned. "His mate?"

She rolled her eyes and brushed out a curl. "Yes, his *mate*. Like Gray is my mate and Maxim is Parker's mate. You know what I'm talking about."

I swallowed and slowly shook my head. "I passed out. He didn't mention anything about a mate, not that I remember, anyway. What does that mean, anyway? Mate? I know you call your boyfriends that, but I just thought it was a shifter term for boyfriend. Does it have another meaning?"

Laila's face turned red and she spun me around in the salon chair to face her. "You don't know?"

I shook my head. "Um, I don't know. Know what? What don't I know?"

"You don't know!" She covered her face with her hands, nearly poking her eye out with a sharp end of a rat tail comb, and groaned. "Oh crap! I'm such a big-mouth. I thought you were just messing around. I am so sorry, Fern. Oh god, just tape my mouth shut."

I took the comb from her and placed it on the counter behind me before someone got hurt. "I don't know what's happening right now. You want to stop and explain?"

"How do you not know about mates? You're raising a shifter."

When I gave her a look, she gasped. "I am so sorry! There I go again with my mouth. I didn't mean it like that. I am going to go play in traffic right now."

"How 'bout you just spit it out instead?"

"Right. Okay. Mates are like...soul *mates*. Shifters have one other person on earth that they connect to on that level. One and only one. Sometimes we never find them, but if we do—when we do—it's like *all* the fireworks and *all* the love sonnets rolled together in one big orgasmic package. It's a love that never grows old and never dies. That's what you and Harrison are. Mates. That feeling you get around him? It's because you're mates."

I laughed. It was ridiculous. Sure, I had feelings for the man, but soul mates? That wasn't a real thing...

"I'm dead serious. You two are mates. He told us last night at the bar. The man is already head over heels for you, that was clear to everyone last night. Think about it. He kept stopping by the salon last week trying to see you. He also went and fetched Kinsley for you from Parker's. By the way, Gray said the two of them looked chummy, which made Gray suspect Harrison might be her accomplice, but that's a story for another day."

I hesitated. "Why didn't I know about this mate thing?"

"Good question. Kinsley's dad never mentioned anything about it?"

"He didn't mention much of anything. He was eighteen and gone by the time I was a few months pregnant. He'd been a senior and a popular high school jock, I'd been an awkward freshman nobody. We met at a party one night and one thing led to another. We only slept together the one time and he only told me what he was because he knew it'd be quite the surprise when Kinsley was born if I'd never heard of shifters."

"What an asshole."

"How... Why me? If it's true, why am I his mate?"

Laila made a face. "Why not? You're great. He's lucky to have a mate like you."

"So, you're telling me that we're fated to be together?"

"Yep. Mates are forever. No matter what. You were destined for each other."

My chest fluttered. "So, sleeping with him wouldn't make me some cheap floozie?"

"No! Even if you weren't mates, it wouldn't. Hello, this is the twenty-first century. Our sisters fought hard during the sexual revolution. Let's not let their sacrifice be in vain."

"Um, you do know the sexual revolution wasn't an actual physical war, right?"

She merely shrugged and continued styling my hair.

"Maybe I should go and talk to him about all of this. Yeah, I need to talk to him."

Laughing, Laila held me down in her chair. "Not until I'm finished with your hair. You're only half-done right now."

The longer I sat in Laila's chair, the more antsy I became. I couldn't stop replaying her words in my head. Harrison was my mate. Forever. Meant to be. He'd known. When he promised me that he wasn't going anywhere, that wasn't an empty promise. He knew. I wondered why he hadn't told me. I wondered how Kinsley was going to react. I wondered what our lives would look like—the three of us.

Kinsley was my main priority. She needed me. She technically needed more than I was able to give her, probably, but I was what she had—all she had. I couldn't lose my focus on that, no matter what. No man came before my child, no matter what kind of soul mate they were.

Soul mate... I moved the word around my mouth, tasting it, muttering it under my breath, trying it on for size. It still felt strange, but Laila was totally right about Harrison. I felt drawn to him like Kinsley was drawn to trouble. Between arguing with my daughter and juggling my disasters, he'd been on my mind in one way or another since I'd met him.

"It's true, Fern. That man is yours and you're his."

I met Laila's eyes in the mirror and gripped the top of my thighs. "I have Kinsley..."

"Now, you have Kinsley and Harrison." She shrugged. "It's just nature. I'd bet you were already taken with the man before I said anything."

I knew my cheeks were turning pink. "What if she doesn't want him to be a part of our family?"

Laila shrugged. "At some point, your own happiness has to matter. Kinsley seems like she's going through that phase where nothing is going to make her happy except making everyone around her miserable. Even so, it sounds like she might be rather fond of Harrison. Gray seemed to think so."

Groaning, I let my head fall back. "Why does everything suddenly feel more complicated than when the two of us were just dating? I guess because you make it sound so serious."

"It is serious. I'd be surprised if you two aren't married six months from now."

"Oh Jesus! Give me a heart attack, why don't you?"

October, who had apparently been eavesdropping, leaned over from her station next to Laila, her long black hair crimped into some wild style atop her head. "I'm going to literally scream if the women around here don't stop bitching when it comes to taking these hot men off the market. First Laila and now you? It sounds to me like you need to stop pussyfooting around, woman, and go claim your man."

18

HARRISON

s I left the clinic for the day, I was surprised to find Fern sitting in her minivan in the parking lot. Her window was down and she peered out at me with a shy smile. "Hey."

I raised my brows. "I was about to head over to your place. What are you doing here?"

"Want to get in?" There was something different about her, something I couldn't place. She seemed slightly out of breath and a little nervous. "I thought we could take a drive."

I rounded the car to the passenger side feeling a little awkward to be letting Fern drive. I didn't want to appear sexist, but there was something about driving my lady around that was akin to caring and providing for her—a natural instinct to a shifter.

"We could take my truck, if you want."

"It'll be a short drive, I promise."

I wasn't going to argue. I was desperate to be near her. If she wanted to pilot me to the moon in her spaceship, I would've hopped into the copilot's seat as long as it meant getting to spend time with her.

I got in and she drove out of the lot heading in the direction of East Public Beach. We only drove for two or three minutes when she parked in a secluded public parking lot behind Cap'n Jim's. We were both quiet. In my case, it was because I was watching her, curious to know what she was up to.

"Close your eyes." She leaned over and stole a quick kiss before getting out of the car. "Keep them closed."

I listened as she opened the back door of the minivan and fiddled around with something. A few minutes passed and then she was back in the front seat, doing something next to me. "What are you up to?"

"Open your eyes."

I did as she said and found that she'd darkened the van by hanging stuff in all the windows but mine. A few towels, a sheet, even what looked like a curtain over the back window. There were also battery-operated tealight candles glowing in the back window. I looked back at her and she had one more towel and some magnetic clamps in her hand that she held out to me.

"Block your window and meet me in the back?"

I was a motivated man, is all I can say. I blocked the window and then hurried out into the rear of the van through the back door. She'd taken out the removable seats and thrown down a comforter that I recognized as the one from her bed. Once we were both inside, I closed the door, looked over at her, and sucked in a deep breath.

She was sitting on her feet and the dress she had on was riding up around her thighs. Her chest heaved as she began what seemed to be a prepared speech. "There is never going to be a perfect time. Kinsley is always going to be home, probably grounded, and I don't even know where you live. I want you, though. I want this. I want us. So, I'm creating a perfect time. Right here, right now...if you want."

If I want? A grin spread across my face. I had to be the luckiest guy on the planet. She was not only adorable, but she'd obviously given this some thought and preparation. What an honor. *If I want?* Hell, yeah, I want.

More animal than man, I lunged for her, grabbing her and pulling her onto my lap. Kissing her hard, I held her too tightly, too desperately. Instead of pulling back, Fern hiked her leg over my thighs so she was straddling me. Her hands were hot on my shoulders as she held onto me.

I stroked the seam of her lips and then into her mouth as she parted them for me. Drinking in the honey taste of her, I deepened the kiss and growled at how good it all was. Running my hand down her back, I cupped her ass and pulled her closer to me, until her core bumped against the straining erection in my jeans.

Fern gasped and let her head fall back, exposing her delicate neck to me. I ran my mouth down her neck and back up again, then nipped her chin. She tasted so good, no matter where my mouth landed. I sucked on her skin and drank in the sounds of her cries of pleasure. Kissing across her collar bones, I pushed the sleeves of her dress down and tasted her shoulders.

Writhing in my lap, she pushed her chest out at me, and I swore before dragging her dress down farther and exposing her breasts to my starving eyes. I buried my face between them and inhaled her scent. The lace of her bra was soft against my skin, but I wanted it gone.

Reading my mind, her hands were already at the hooks, undoing it. I pulled the bra out of the way and growled low in my throat. Perfect breasts with dark-pink nipples waited for me. Full, round, and heavy, they filled my hands. Running my thumbs over her nipples, I lowered my mouth to them. Licking, biting, and sucking, I teased her until her hips rocked against me. Her hands were lodged in my hair, and each hard pull on her sensitive flesh earned me a hard tug on my hair.

I worked my hand between us and cupped her hot core through her panties. As she rocked her hips, I pressed my palm against her clit and let her ride my hand. Little gasps and mewls flooded the car as she worked herself higher and higher. Just when she was about to come undone, I slipped my hand away and gave her nipples one last lick.

"Harrison..."

I grinned at my mate and slowly worked her dress up her thighs. "I promise it'll be worth the wait, honey."

She grabbed the hem of my shirt and yanked it up. I had to let go of her dress while she tore my shirt off, but when her hands went to my belt, I lost my playful spirit. I pulled her dress over her head and tossed it aside. Seeing her straddling me with nothing on but a pair of lacey white panties just about did me in.

I didn't want to be rough with her, but I needed to feel her around me. I ripped her cute little panties off and slid my thumb through her wetness. She was drenched for me, that honey dripping down her thighs. I wanted to drag her up and lick her clean, but we were both too far gone.

"Later. I'm going to taste this pussy later."

Fern's cheeks burned red and I watched in fascination as it trailed down her neck and chest, all the way down to the tips of her pink nipples. She yanked at my belt and growled. "I can't get this off."

"You had no problem the other night."

She cupped me through my pants and let out a desperate sigh. "Pull your pants down."

I shoved my pants down as far as I could get them with her in my lap, but it was enough to get my dick out. I swore worse than a sailor as her hand wrapped around me and started tugging up and down. "Need to be in you."

"Do it." She let go of me and dug her fingers into my shoulders, readying herself.

I stroked through her wetness and teased her opening, needing to be sure she was able to take me. Pushing one finger in, then another, I fucked her that way while she moaned and worked her hips up and down. It would be tight, but I couldn't wait any longer. Lining our bodies up, I ran her wetness over myself and then slowly pushed into her.

My entire world narrowed until all that existed was her, on top of me, breathily begging me for more. Inch by excruciating inch, I pushed inside of her until our bodies fit together so tightly that not even a piece of paper could've fit between us. She squeezed around me, her body molding perfectly to mine.

Clinging to me, Fern suddenly let out a breathy laugh. "I shouldn't have waited so long to do this."

Groaning, I slid out and thrust back home. "You were waiting for someone who would cherish you the way you deserve. You were waiting for me."

She peppered kisses on my mouth and neck as I pumped in and out of her eager body. Her hands tangled in my hair, and she moaned as she pressed her chest flush against mine. "So…good."

I gripped her ass and took her with all the need I felt for her. Harder and faster, until the car was filled with her cries. I growled her name and held on through the need to sink my teeth into her neck, marking her as mine.

Fern's body squeezed around my shaft, pulsing, gripping me over and over, as she threw her head back and let out a wild scream. Her body shook as her orgasm overtook her. Mine followed just behind and I felt my very soul attempt to leave my body to be in hers. Gripping her hard, I fought the urge to mark her. Not until she agreed to it.

As the strongest orgasm I'd ever felt crashed through me, I knew that life as I had known it was forever changed. There was never going to be a day when I didn't think of how it felt to have my mate come apart in my arms. There would never be a day when I didn't desperately want to hear her cry out my name.

I gripped her hair and lifted her head so I could kiss her. Hungry, still starving for her, I poured everything I couldn't say into that kiss. Everything she probably wasn't ready to hear from me, everything that was too soon to say, everything I'd felt for her since the moment I saw her. I forced it all into that one kiss. A declaration, or a warning, I wasn't sure. Fern was mine. I was hers.

She kissed me back just as fiercely and only pulled back to look into my eyes with a declaration of her own. "Mate."

19

FERN

*T*he air conditioner was running, but it wasn't enough to combat the heat we created. A droplet of sweat rolled down between my shoulder blades, but I was too spent to move. I never wanted to move again.

Harrison held me, wrapped tightly in his big arms. The beat of his heart was strong and steady against my cheek, his breath gentle as it ruffled the top of my hair. "I should've told you sooner."

It'd been several silent minutes since I'd said the word that was still hanging in the air between us. Mate. That's what we were. After being with him physically, I knew it with crystal clarity. He was still hard inside me, our bodies still connected. I was his and he was mine.

"I can't blame you. I'm not sure I would have believed you. It's crazy."

"But you do believe it?" He rubbed my back. "You better believe it after what we just did. I don't know if there was a better way to show you."

I kissed the side of his neck and sighed. "I believe it. I wouldn't mind you showing me again a few thousand more times, though."

Laughing, he ran his hand up to the back of my neck and held me even more tightly. "At least a few thousand more times. In the next year alone. There are all kinds of things I have in mind for you."

"It still feels completely off the wall. I never knew anything about mates. To say my mind is blown is an understatement." As reality started to slowly seep between us, I wiggled off him so it wouldn't be as awkward when I brought up my kid. "With Kinsley…things are complicated. I don't think I can just bring you into our lives fully until she's more prepared."

He pulled me back into his arms and kissed me. "We'll figure it out."

"If you were smart, you'd run." I held his gaze and felt my chest tighten at the warning I just gave him. I was only half kidding. "Kinsley is never going to be easy, at least not for the next five or six years. She has these moments when she looks at me and I think she wants to murder me in my sleep. There are fights. Always. And when there isn't fighting, there's the silent treatment. Some days, it goes from an inferno to an igloo in that house fast, I suffer frostbite.

And it's not just her. It's easy to point the finger at the screaming, cursing teenager, but it's me, too. I get stressed and fight back when I shouldn't and say things I regret. I let her get away with things sometimes because I'm too tired to stop her."

"I'll help."

"I'm not supposed to let a man I barely know into our family like this. There are entire childcare books about it and it's advice I've always heeded."

"I'm not some random man you barely know. I'm your mate. I would do anything for you, and I would do anything for Kinsley. I will fight to the death to protect both of you if I have to. I'll damn sure fight to make sure that you're both happy."

I bit my lip. "Can we still take it slow?"

He looked down at my nude body and arched a brow.

"Not that part. I mean the part about bringing you into our family. If we ease you in, maybe it won't be as big a deal for Kinsley."

"Whatever you want. I'll let you set the pace on this and I'll follow your lead. I'll do anything you ask in order to make this easier for you. The fact is, I'll do anything to be a family with you and Kinsley."

I buried my face in his chest to hide the stupid smile that insisted on stretching my lips across my face. My life suddenly felt exciting and, dare I say, *fun*? Wrapped in Harrison's arms in the back of a hot minivan, I felt like things were going to be okay. More than okay, exhilarating.

"Where is Kinsley now?"

"Home. She had homework to do. I told her I was running to Laila's and I'd be back in a few minutes, hoping she wouldn't be bold enough to sneak out." I sighed. "I need to get back."

"So, you snuck out to see me?"

I grinned up at him. "Like a teenager."

He adjusted me on his lap until our bodies were lined up again and pulled me down on his shaft. He kissed my moan away and used his grip on my hips to rock my body against his, reaching my most sensitive spots. "Just one more time."

I kissed him back, stroking his tongue with my own. "One more and then I have to go."

He slipped his hand between us and found my clit with his fingers as his hips started working under me, filling me slow and hard. "I better make it count, then."

It was getting dark when we finished, and I dropped him off back at the clinic parking lot. He pulled me out of the car and we made out against the side of his truck while traffic went by on Main Street. I was on cloud nine as I drove home, unable to wipe the smile off my face. Every moment with Harrison made that mate bond thing between us stronger. It was like a tangible connection I could feel tugging at me as I drove away.

I was already plotting our next covert meetup when I pulled into my driveway and hurried inside the house. I planned to check on Kinsley and Boots and then climb into bed and replay every second of what just happened.

Still grinning from ear to ear, I knocked on Kinsley's bedroom door and pushed it open when she didn't answer. "Hey, Kinsley?"

What greeted me was an empty room. Swearing, I searched the rest of the house and then checked the yard to see if she was maybe outside somewhere. She wasn't. Boots was whining in his crate, so I let him outside while I paced trying to figure out where my daughter might've gone.

The weight of my reality settled heavily on my shoulders, and I couldn't help playing the same self-deprecating thoughts in my head that re-emerged anytime I took a selfish moment to myself. I'd been out getting laid instead of home parenting my child. Frustration built in my chest and bubbled up until it lodged in my throat. It always felt bad, but this time, it felt much worse than usual after the happiness I'd just experienced being with Harrison.

As soon as Boots had done his business, I carried him back inside and let him run free through the house while I went back into Kinsley's room. I hardly ever ventured inside her bedroom, but I was stressed and angry and wanted an answer as to where she might have gone.

Hoping something on her desk would give me a clue, I sat in her chair and started rifling through things. Notebooks full of school work, random drawings of wolves and bears, even a couple of little doodles of hearts with two sets of initials drawn in them, but nothing that was any help in determining her whereabouts. I started opening her desk drawers but stopped instantly when I saw what was inside the bottom drawer.

My heart beat so hard that it rang in my ears. There, inside her drawer, was a baggie with little white pills. I sucked in a sharp breath and picked up the small plastic bag. My world narrowed into tunnel vision and that bag was the only thing I could see. I didn't need to be a detective to know what I was holding in my hands. My child, my fifteen-year-old daughter, had some type of illicit drugs in her possession.

Shock and fury washed over me and I stood so fast that the chair flew back into the wall and the force knocked a few precariously shelved knickknacks off the bookcase. I was angry at my child for having drugs, but I was angrier that someone had given my child drugs. I didn't even know what the pills were exactly. There was still the tiny voice in my head that whispered maybe they were an oddly shaped acetaminophen or ibuprofen or some other over-the-counter medication. And maybe they just happened to be in a baggie because the original container had been damaged. And maybe my daughter was suffering from headaches or a head cold or something that would warrant her having OTC meds. But I knew better. She didn't get headaches. As a shifter, she hadn't been sick a single day in her fifteen years of life. Whatever else the pills were, they were most certainly bad news.

Reeling, I stormed out of the house and started calling Kinsley's name. My entire body felt numb. I stumbled over my feet and only barely regained my balance in time to keep from falling flat on my face.

I called out one last time in complete desperation. Then, I spotted her. She was leaning against a car a few houses down, staring at me with a scowl on her face. It seemed as though her temper was seething, too. Mine was worse. Much, much worse.

I glowered at the older boys she was standing with and grabbed her arm. "Get home right now."

She yanked her arm out of my grasp and stepped back. "What is your problem?"

It was then that I realized I was still holding the bag of pills. I thrust it angrily in her face. "This. This is my problem. Get home, now."

20

FERN

Kinsley marched home in front of me. I could tell the gears in her head were grinding and she was preparing for a monstrous blow up by the way her hands kept fisting and unfisting at her sides. If she thought she was going to win the fight we were about to have, she had another thing coming. She stomped up the stairs and tried to slam the door in my face, but caught my shoulder instead. Instead of apologizing for hitting me, she merely stomped off into her room.

"Get back here!" I followed her, rubbing my aching shoulder.

"What the fuck did you do to my room?!" she screeched and backed out of her room, glaring at me. "You destroyed it!"

"What are you doing with drugs, Kinsley?"

"What were you doing in my room?"

"You left this house when I told you not to. Then I find *drugs* in your room? What the hell were you thinking?" I paced back and forth in front of the short hallway leading to her bedroom. "Drugs, Kinsley? I know you've got a vicious mouth on you, and I know you're moody and dealing with a lot of difficult physical changes right now. I know you're adapting to a new town and a new school and new friends, but goddammit, Kinsley, I thought you were smarter than this!"

96

"I'm not even going to bother trying to explain myself because you won't even listen to me! All you do is lecture and act disappointed all the time." She tried to slam her bedroom door shut, but I shoved my foot in the way. "Get out of my room!"

"No! You are not running away from me tonight. You and I are going to talk. I don't care how long it takes. We're going to talk about this, and you're going to explain to me why the hell you have drugs in your room."

"Oh, like you even care. Your life would be so much easier without me in it. Then, you could just run off with your new boyfriend and have a new family, and everything would be so much easier for you, wouldn't it?"

I gripped her door as she tried to push me out. "My life would be easier if you didn't fight with me about every single thing! It would be easier if my own daughter didn't hate me!"

"I saw you tonight. I saw you drop *him* off at the clinic. I saw you two sucking face. How do you think I feel about that? You don't even care! You don't care about anything but yourself!"

"Bullshit! That's bullshit and you know it, Kinsley!"

"Oh, that's right, my bad. You care about *him*!" Kinsley gave up trying to shut the door and stormed across her room, trashing the stuff on top of her desk. "You've got a new boyfriend and that's all that matters, right?"

"You're not even making any sense. You matter to me. You staying off drugs and having a good life matters to me."

"What. Ever. You lied to me tonight. You said you were going to Laila's and I saw you sucking face with Dr. Daniels. You smell like a slut, too. You're an embarrassment."

"My dating Harrison is bothering you this much?"

"Yes! It is!"

My heart lurched in my chest, but I ignored it. It didn't matter. Keeping my daughter safe did. "Fine. I won't see him anymore."

"What?" Kinsley had a book in her hand and was preparing to throw it across the room. She paused mid throw and stared at me with a disgusted look on her face.

"I said I won't see him anymore. If it will stop you from acting out and hurting yourself with toxic substances, I won't see him anymore."

"How could you even say that? How could you do that to him? He's your mate and you'd just throw him away like that?"

My head was spinning. "How do you…"

"I know things! I know that he's your mate and you'd just toss him aside. You don't deserve him. You're so selfish!"

"You listen to me, Kinsley Maude Day. The moment I found out I was pregnant with you, when I was fifteen years old, I have thought of nothing but you. When my parents kicked me out and I had nowhere to go, I worried about how I would keep you safe. I worried about how I would support and protect you. I worried about how I would provide for you. The same things I've worried about every day since. I've scrimped and saved and sacrificed—all for you. Every. Single. Day. Since I was your age.

"And I'll tell you something else. I'd do it again in a heartbeat because I love you. I love you even though you treat me like I'm a thorn in your side. Even when you tell me how much you hate me. So don't you dare call me selfish, young lady. I never claimed to be perfect and I have a lot of faults, I know that, but selfishness in not one of them. For the last fifteen years, I have been anything but selfish.

"As for Harrison, he *is* my mate and I was with him tonight. I like him. I want to be with him. But if you're going to throw your life down the toilet because of it, I'll give him up. From the day you were born, you've been my number one. My priority is to keep you safe. I think the best thing to do here is for me to quit my job and we'll move. We'll go somewhere and start fresh. Somewhere you can get away from the friends you have now—the bad influences."

"What?! Are you kidding me?!" Kinsley headed toward the front door, shoving me out of her path. "I hate you!"

I tried to hold onto her, but as a shifter, she was so much stronger than I was, and she shoved me away again. "Kinsley, stop!"

"I'm not leaving Sunkissed Key. I'm never leaving. You can't ruin my life all over again. You leave if you want, but I'm not going. If you could make it on your own at fifteen, so can I. I don't need you."

One more strong shove from her and I fell back against the wall. While I was trying to get my feet under me, she ran out of the room. Chasing after her, I yelled and begged her to stop, but nothing worked. She ran out of the house and down the steps. By the time I got to the street, she was already gone.

I ran up and down the street, calling her name, asking people if they'd seen her. I jogged up and down Shipwreck Way. I walked up and down Main Street. I searched for her in every place I thought she would be, but I couldn't find her.

I wasn't sure how long it'd been, or what time it was, but I was a mess by the time I got back to the house. I was physically and emotionally beat. Sobbing, I found my phone and dialed the one person I knew I could count on, no matter what. Sucking in a deep breath, I tried to compose myself before Harrison picked up.

"Hey, honey. Everything good?"

"No. Kinsley ran away." A sob broke free and a fresh batch of tears poured down my cheeks. I fought through the sobs to tell Harrison what had happened. "We fought. We fought and she ran away. I've been looking for her, but I can't find her. I can't find her anywhere, Harrison. She's gone."

"She's not gone, honey. I'm on my way. I'll find her, okay?"

"Please find her. Please."

21

HARRISON

*I*t took me less than ten minutes to track Kinsley down. When I knocked on the front door of the three-story beachfront home on Flamingo Lane, I was seething with anger. My bear wanted to tear something apart. Hearing Fern cry like that just about gutted me. Knowing she was at home, terrified and devastated, had me on the verge of an uncontrolled shift.

A teenage boy answered the door, a smirk on his face. "What's up, Dr. Daniels? Come to check my temperature?"

I grabbed him by the back of his shirt collar, lifting him off the ground as I barged into the house. Holding the struggling teen in the air, I walked from room to room and growled loudly. "Kinsley, you'd better get out here right now before I make a light snack of your boyfriend."

"Let me down! Let me down, or I'm going to tell my father about this!"

I shook the little shithead once and glared into his frightened eyes. "How old are you? Eighteen, nineteen? Kinsley is fifteen. She ran away from home. If her mother knew you were holding her here, she could press charges against you. Keep running your mouth and I'll make sure she does."

Kinsley popped up from behind the couch in the formal living room and, red faced, marched over to me. "She didn't have to send you."

"Did you hear her calling you?" I was so angry that I had to force myself to loosen my grip on the asshole in my hand before I strangled him. "Did you?"

"Well, yeah, but—"

"Outside. Get outside right now. We have some talking to do about what a selfish, rotten thing you just did to your mother. Hiding from her while she was calling you, scared out of her wits that something might happen to you... You should be ashamed of yourself. And this is your choice of boyfriend? Really? Uh-uh. No. Not going to work."

"You're not my fucking dad!"

"And you're damn lucky. If I *were* your dad, you'd be doing chores every day after school until bedtime for the next three months while I hover over you like a drill sergeant." I shook my head at her, dropped her boyfriend on the ground, and got an inch from his face. "Stay away from her. If I catch you around her again, I'll break every bone in your body. Understand?"

Kinsley stormed out onto the porch and started down the stairs to the beach. I was right behind her, trying to decide what I could and couldn't say. I was so angry that I finally decided to throw caution to the wind.

"What the hell happened?"

"Oh, she didn't tell you? She called you so fast that I figured she would have already given you the play by play and sucked your face off by now."

I grabbed her by the arms. Glaring down at her, I let my bear flash into my face. "You don't talk about your mother like that. I don't know everything about the relationship between you two, but I know that she loves you more than anything in the world. I know that she works herself ragged providing for you. She would rather lose her mate than hurt you. So you watch your mouth and remember who you're talking about. I know you're angry, but that woman deserves your respect."

She sagged against me, all anger suddenly gone out of her. "I'm sorry."

"Don't apologize to me. Apologize to her. She called me, sobbing hysterically. She's scared to death that you're in danger."

"I didn't mean for any of this to happen. She found the Xannies in my room and I knew she wasn't going to listen. I just got so angry. I don't even know what I was saying when I was yelling at her, but *she* was yelling, too. Then she told me we were going to move again. She wants to move away from here. I don't want to move. It sucks being the noob—starting a new school in a new town with no friends. Is she just going to keep making me leave my home every time I do something she doesn't like?"

"Xannies—You mean Xanax?" I swallowed back an urge to vomit at the idea of Fern leaving Sunkissed Key. I couldn't think about that at the moment. I wouldn't let that happen anyway. "So, you were in possession of drugs—illicit prescription benzodiazepines?"

"Oh, she didn't tell you?"

I sighed. "Come on. We can talk when we get you home to your mom."

"I don't want to go back there. She's furious."

Staring down at Kinsley, it wasn't hard to see the mixed-up, struggling kid in her. She was lashing out and making dumb choices, but she was just a kid. "She's not furious. She's scared. She's just trying to keep you safe. I don't have kids, so I don't know what it's like personally, but I see parents in my office all the time. They're all just scared, Kinsley. Raising a kid isn't easy, and it doesn't come with a rule book. Your mom's been doing it on her own."

"I'm not stupid, though. She doesn't have to worry about me so much. I'm not going to get knocked up like she did. I don't do drugs and I don't drink because there's no real point."

"Then why did you have the drugs?" I led her down Main Street and back toward her house. I was feeling a little guilty for not calling Fern right away, but I thought it was important to talk to Kinsley first and calm her down before she faced off with Fern.

"They weren't mine. I took them from...someone. So they wouldn't do them."

"That boyfriend of yours?"

She looked away. "He's not that bad."

"He's never coming near you again. He's dead meat if he does. He's too old, too stupid, and too much of an asshat." I shook my head. "That relationship is over. Sorry, kid."

"Is this what it's going to be like? You and my mom sneaking off to be together and then you bossing me around and trying to control my life?"

I grunted. "You knew we snuck off together, huh?"

"Like I said, I'm not stupid."

"It made you mad?"

She grunted back at me. "It's stupid that she tried to hide it from me."

"That's why you're upset? Not because she's with me?"

Scowling, Kinsley rolled her eyes and looked away. "I don't care if she's with you. You're mates. I get it."

On Magnolia Street, Kinsley let out a groan when she saw her house and Fern sitting on the porch, wringing her hands and looking distraught. I held the back of her neck and squeezed lightly, giving her support. "You're her world. Remember that."

Fern was up and running toward us the second she saw us. She grabbed her daughter and pulled her against her chest, holding her tightly. "I'm going to murder you later, but right now, I'm just so glad to see you. I love you, Kinsley. I love you so much. Don't you ever run off like that again."

Kinsley groaned and made a weak attempt at pushing her mother away. When I caught a glimpse of her face over Fern's shoulder, though, I saw tears in the girl's eyes.

"Thank you, Harrison." Fern finally let her daughter go and stepped back. "I'm sorry we bothered you."

I gestured toward the house. "I think Kinsley has something she wants to tell you."

Kinsley snarled at me, as though that would intimidate me. I snarled right back, and Kinsley turned and slunk inside. I followed closely behind her, not giving Fern a chance to dismiss me. I knew she wanted to take it slow, but I wasn't leaving. They both needed me.

Inside, Kinsley threw herself on the couch dramatically and crossed her arms, preparing for whatever was coming. I sat next to her, and Boots ran over and sat at my feet, waiting for me to scratch him behind his ears.

22

FERN

When I entered the house, Kinsley, Harrison, and Boots were already sitting on the couch together. I stopped short. It was the picture-perfect family, and seeing it like that was a blow to the gut. Especially since I couldn't have it. Not after the fight with Kinsley. I didn't know how to tell Harrison to leave, though, especially not when I wanted him there so badly.

"I'm sorry." Kinsley blurted out the apology and groaned. "I shouldn't have said all that stuff and I shouldn't have run away. The Xannies weren't mine, though. I took them to stop my boyfriend from using them, and I just put them in my desk without thinking. You were mad for no reason."

Harrison cleared his throat.

Kinsley glared at him. "But I'm still sorry."

I sat in the chair across from them and rested with my elbows on my knees. "Your *boyfriend*?"

Harrison snorted. "*Ex*-boyfriend. It's over."

"No, it's not."

"Yes, it is. I meant what I said to him. If he comes around you again, and I'll know if he does, I will tear him limb from limb and toss his remains into the Atlantic Ocean."

"Mom, he can't do that!"

Harrison snorted again. "As a concerned citizen, I can and will do that. He's an asshat."

I held up my hands. "You met him?"

"That's where I found her. He's a punk—not nearly good enough for her."

Kinsley stared him down for a few more seconds and then shrugged and slumped back on the couch. "What. Ever. I was going to break up with him anyway."

I released a slow breath. "You had a boyfriend."

"It's not a big deal, Mom. It wasn't serious."

I looked at Harrison. "You'll really get rid of him if he bothers her?"

He nodded with a grin. "It would be my pleasure."

I sat back in my chair. My thoughts were spinning too fast for me to fully process. "But those weren't your pills?"

"No, Mom. I don't do drugs."

Apparently, there was a lot I didn't know. I rubbed my face and sighed. "We can't keep doing this, Kinsley. I can't keep fighting with you like this. I'm tired and I'm very near my breaking point."

"Fine. Then, we won't fight. I don't want to leave Sunkissed Key, though. I want to stay."

I looked at Harrison and found him watching me with a curious expression on his handsome face. I looked back at Kinsley. "I don't want to leave, either. But make no mistake, if I think you're getting into trouble and I need to leave for your safety or protection, I will move us out of here so fast, your head will spin like the exorcist. I don't care whether it's what you want or not, Kinsley. I will do anything I have to do to keep you safe."

"Including leaving your mate?"

Kinsley's question pierced my heart like a blade. I looked at my feet and felt tears prick my eyes. Of course, I didn't want to leave him. In the little time I'd known him, he'd become a huge part of my life. Like tonight. He was the one I called. He'd come to the rescue and found her for me. He'd walked her home and, oddly, he'd both threatened and comforted her. I saw the way she relaxed around him. Whether she knew it or not, she liked him, too.

"That's not an option." Harrison's deep growl was more of a rattle through the room than anything resembling a normal human voice. "There's nowhere you could go that I wouldn't follow."

I snapped my head around to him and found him staring at me with a burning intensity. I opened my mouth to argue, but found that I didn't want to.

"I didn't mean what I said earlier." Kinsley's voice was quiet. "I was just mad that you tried to hide it from me when you went out with him. It sucks when you treat me like a child. I don't care if you're sleeping together. I just don't like being lied to."

"Kinsley..." I swallowed back the embarrassment of the situation and nodded. "You're right. I shouldn't have lied to you and I'm sorry."

Harrison captured her attention. "I want to be here for both of you. I want your mom in my life, and I want you in my life, despite the fact that you're kind of a pain in my ass, Miss Rude 'Tude."

Kinsley smirked. "Har har, Dr. Harry Bear."

"Good one. Very clever." Harrison grinned and shook his head before he continued. "What I don't want to do is upset you—or your mom—or make anything harder for you. So, what would work for you? What do you want?"

My breath caught in my throat as I waited for Kinsley's answer. My heart pounded away, and the butterflies in my stomach went crazy. I wanted to cry. Harrison had done the perfect thing to make me fall for him that much more. He was treating Kinsley the way she wanted to be treated, asking her point-blank. It was bold and kind and scary as hell.

"This. We're all talking and it's okay."

He smiled at her. "I told you about mates. I want to be with your mom more than I've ever wanted anything in my life. I'm going to do everything I can to make her happy and keep her smiling for as long as I live. What I didn't tell you, and what I didn't know until I met you two, is that the mate bond extends to every part of your mom. Even you. I know that I'm never going to be your dad, but I am your mom's mate. And you are your mom's daughter, so by default, you're mine, too. And unlike your dad, I *do* want to be here. I *do* want to be a part of your life. I want to make sure you're happy, too."

I was crying. I couldn't help it. There wasn't a single thing he could have said that would have been more perfect.

Kinsley cleared her throat and looked away from us. When she looked back at Harrison, she shrugged. "You're kind of a pain in the ass, too. You're bossy, and if you think you're going to tell me who I can and can't date, you're wrong. You're always nagging about how I talk to Mom, but Boots likes you a lot. I guess it wouldn't be too awful if you were around."

Harrison laughed. "I'll remind you that you said that a few months from now when you're mad at me."

"If you're going to be around, I want something out of it, though."

"Kinsley—" I started to chastise her, but Harrison cut me off.

"Name your price."

"I want a car when I'm sixteen. You're a doctor, you've got money. You can buy me a car."

"That's hilarious."

"I'm serious." She crossed her arms over her chest again and frowned. "You're going to be around all the time, you're going to be rubbing your stinky bear scent all over my mom, you'll probably be eating all of the good snacks and leaving the toilet seat up. I deserve a car, at least."

"I'll give you shifter lessons and buy you a bicycle."

"As many shifter lessons as I want. And a golf cart."

"As many shifter lessons as you want and a scooter."

"Ugh. Fuck it. I'll take the bike."

"Kinsley! Language." I rested my head in my hand. The whole night had gotten away from me entirely.

"Geeze, Mom. It's just a word." She looked at me sheepishly. "Am I still grounded?"

"Oh yes. Big time."

"Mom! Seriously?"

"Yes, seriously. Hugely, enormously grounded. You should go to your room now and start cleaning it, actually."

"What the hell? When we live with Harrison, I want a separate part of the house completely. I want my own wing of the house. The west wing." She picked up Boots and carried him with her. "I can't believe you're still going to ground me, after I said I was okay with Harry Bear hanging around."

Harrison growled. "That's *Doctor* Harry Bear, thank you."

It was the damnedest thing. I could've sworn I saw my morose, sullen child crack a smile before disappearing into her room.

Once her door slammed, I met Harrison's gaze and watched as he patted the couch next to him. Shaking my head, I squinted and furrowed my brow. "I feel like you and my daughter just made a lot of decisions for me."

He slowly stood up and walked over to me. Kneeling in front of me, he rested his hands on my thighs. "Fate made a lot of decisions for you. We just helped it along."

"I don't know if I can do any of this, Harrison." I sighed. "I want to, but what if I can't? What if I can't balance it all?"

"You don't have to. It's not all on you anymore. I'm here to help."

"So, what? You just move in and we live happily ever after?"

"Honestly, my house is bigger. Not big enough for Kinsley to have her own wing, but she can have a room far enough away that she won't hear us. My house also has an alarm system, you know, for the times she tries to sneak out." He shrugged. "After you move in, we can get married if you want, or just live like heathens. Have another baby, if you want, or just enjoy that ball of sweetness you already have. I don't care, as long as you're by my side."

I choked. "What?"

"There's the claiming mark, too. It's like getting married for shifters. It's a bite, but not a painful one. I received a disgustingly long, detailed lecture about it from my parents when I was younger, so I can assure you, I'll make it pleasant. I'd love for you to meet my parents, too. They don't come down too often, but maybe we can have them over for Thanksgiving? My mom is going to adore having Kinsley to spoil."

Slapping his shoulder, I stood up and gasped when he pulled me back down.

"I'm teasing you. It's all going to happen, but there's no rush. We're in this for the long haul, honey. You and me. No matter what you were thinking earlier, you're not getting rid of me. Ever."

"I don't know whether to laugh or cry."

He cupped my cheek and smiled. "Do whatever you need to do. I'll be right here beside you through it all."

Launching myself into his arms, we both fell backward, hitting the coffee table and sending it skidding across the floor into the wall. The noise was ridiculous, but Kinsley didn't come out of her room. Spread out on top of him, I laughed. "You have no idea yet what you're committing to."

His kiss was soft and tender. "Whatever it is, I'm all in."

23

KINSLEY

I pulled myself up out of the water with my arms and headed for the nearest lounge chair, dripping pool water across the smooth cement. My towel was draped over the chair. I wrapped it around me and adjusted my sunglasses in the hot sun as I looked around for Boots. The little furball was curled up under a palm tree taking an afternoon snooze.

It had been two months since Mom and Harrison had officially mated and we'd moved into Harrison's ginormous house. When I told him I wanted my own wing, I'd been kidding, but that's almost what I got. I ended up with a huge bedroom that had a bathroom and sliding doors to a balcony that faced the ocean. Seriously sweet.

The house was right on the beach with two wrap around porches, a swimming pool, and a family room with a massive TV and a pool table. With this awesome house, including my decked out bedroom and private bathroom, being grounded around here was not bad. Not bad at all.

I didn't mind my friends seeing me at the Children's Clinic anymore since the town pediatrician was now my stepfather. In fact, I hung out there a lot. Polly was actually kinda cool, and she was also a shifter. Harrison and Polly both agreed that next month, when I turned sixteen, I could have a job there. Harrison suggested I work a few days a week in the summer and on Saturday mornings during the school year, but I had to promise not to threaten any of the kids. No problem there, especially since he'd mentioned nothing at all about snarling at the flirty moms who eye-screwed him. Those bitches better watch out.

After drying off, I strolled into the house to get a snack from the kitchen. My mom and Harrison were in there. Mom was leaning against the island giggling. Harrison had his arm around her was and kissing her neck. *Ugh! Again?*

I cleared my throat. "Um, excuse me. I was just looking for a knife."

Harrison motioned with his head. "In the drawer."

My mom's eyes narrowed. "What do you need a knife for, Kinsley?

"So I can gouge my eyes out! If you two horny toads keep at it, there's going to be sleepless nights, crying babies and stinky diapers around here in another nine months."

My mom blushed, but Harrison grinned from ear to ear and kissed her lightly on the forehead. "Let me guess, you're feeding the bottom-less pit again, Rude 'Tude?"

"Hey, you're the one who told me I wouldn't get fat, Harry Bear." I pried open an air tight container with homemade chocolate chip cookies from Grandma Dot and grabbed myself a handful.

That was another thing. I also had grandparents now—for the first time ever. Harrison's parents, Walter and Dorothea Daniels, lived near Tampa but had come to visit a couple times already. Dorothea made me call them Grandma Dot and Grandpa Wally. Harrison said his mom was over the moon because she finally had a grandchild. I kind of liked having a Grandma Dot, too, even though, in addition to the cookies, she kept sending me weird crocheted sweaters.

"So, my sixteenth birthday is next month—"

"Is it?" Harrison pretended to be surprised, but I was on to him. He knew. He was a bad actor.

"Anyhow, I was wondering if I could have a pool party here."

Harrison and mom exchanged glances and both of them grinned

like they had something up their sleeves. I wasn't sure what, but something.

My mom met my eyes and winked at me. "I think that might work. As long as you behave and don't get yourself grounded. We can start making plans this weekend."

It was interesting seeing the changes in Mom. She was way happier and less stressed with Harrison around. I watched as they left the kitchen. Sometimes those two were in their own little world. Harrison's arm was still around mom, and her head leaned on him as they walked. I didn't ask where they were going because I was pretty sure I already knew and I really didn't want the mental picture invading my thoughts. There wasn't enough Clorox bleach on Sunkissed Key to clean that vision out of my brain.

I would deny it to my mom or Harrison, but I secretly wouldn't mind being a big sister. It would be cool having a little rug rat running around here, especially if my little brother or sister was a shifter, too.

And as for my sixteenth birthday, I'm still working on getting that car.

THE END

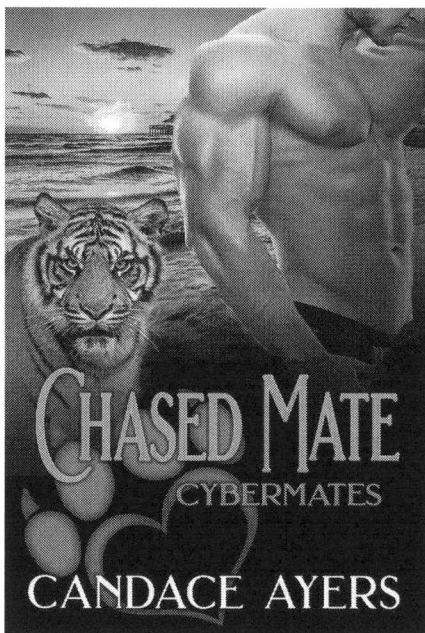

Arden Richardson has no excuse.
She doesn't know why she does it.
The comatose man isn't even her patient.
But...
Her kiss awakens the sleeping giant.

Flynn Bennett has a shady past.
It extends back almost to the cradle.
He's trouble with a capital T.
But...
One kiss is all it takes...

The bad boy.
The ex-con.
The bootlegger.

NEXT BOOK IN THIS SERIES...

Vows to be a better man—for her...

The beauty.
The nurse.
His mate.

Get Chased Mate HERE

P.O.L.A.R.

P.O.L.A.R. (*Private Ops: League Arctic Rescue*) *is a specialized, private operations task force—a maritime unit of polar bear shifters. Part of a worldwide, clandestine army comprised of the best of the best shifters, P.O.L.A.R.'s home base is Siberia...until the team pisses somebody off and gets re-assigned to Sunkissed Key, Florida and these arctic shifters suddenly find themselves surrounded by sun, sand, flip-flops and palm trees.*

1. Rescue Bear
2. Hero Bear
3. Covert Bear
4. Tactical Bear
5. Royal Bear

BEARS OF BURDEN

In the southwestern town of Burden, Texas, good ol' bears Hawthorne, Wyatt, Hutch, Sterling, and Sam, and Matt are livin' easy. Beer flows freely, and pretty women are abundant. The last thing the shifters of Burden are thinking about is finding a mate or settling down. But, fate has its own plan...

1. Thorn
2. Wyatt
3. Hutch
4. Sterling
5. Sam
6. Matt

SHIFTERS OF HELL'S CORNER

In the late 1800's, on a homestead in New Mexico, a female shifter named Helen Cartwright, widowed under mysterious circumstances, knew there was power in the feminine bonds of sisterhood. She provided an oasis for those like herself, women who had been dealt the short end of the stick. Like magic, women have flocked to the tiny town of Helen's Corner ever since. Although, nowadays, some call the town by another name, ***Hell's Crazy Corner.***

1. Wolf Boss
2. Wolf Detective
3. Wolf Soldier
4. Bear Outlaw
5. Wolf Purebred

DRAGONS OF THE BAYOU

Something's lurking in the swamplands of the Deep South. Massive creatures exiled from their home. For each, his only salvation is to find his one true mate.

1. Fire Breathing Beast
2. Fire Breathing Cezar
3. Fire Breathing Blaise
4. Fire Breathing Remy
5. Fire Breathing Armand
6. Fire Breathing Ovide

RANCHER BEARS

When the patriarch of the Long family dies, he leaves a will that has each of his five son's scrambling to find a mate. Underneath it all, they find that family is what matters most.

1. Rancher Bear's Baby
2. Rancher Bear's Mail Order Mate
3. Rancher Bear's Surprise Package
4. Rancher Bear's Secret
5. Rancher Bear's Desire
6. Rancher Bears' Merry Christmas

Rancher Bears Complete Box Set

KODIAK ISLAND SHIFTERS

On Port Ursa in Kodiak Island Alaska, the Sterling brothers are kind of a big deal.
They own a nationwide chain of outfitter retail stores that they grew from their father's little backwoods camping supply shop.
The only thing missing from the hot bear shifters' lives are mates! But, not for long...

1. Billionaire Bear's Bride (COLTON)
2. The Bear's Flamingo Bride (WYATT)
3. Military Bear's Mate (TUCKER)

SHIFTERS OF DENVER

Nathan: Billionaire Bear- A matchmaker meets her match.
Byron: Heartbreaker Bear- A sexy heartbreaker with eyes for just one woman.
Xavier: Bad Bear - She's a good girl. He's a bad bear.

1. Nathan: Billionaire Bear
2. Byron: Heartbreaker Bear
3. Xavier: Bad Bear

Shifters of Denver Complete Box Set

Printed in Great Britain
by Amazon